"Gage, I don't know how to thank you."

"I have a suggestion. Have dinner with me."

"I don't know."

He placed the last decoration on her tree, finding a bare spot. "We've become friends and I'd like to take you out."

"My life is really complicated. And I haven't been on a date in a long time. It isn't fair going out with some nice guy when I have all of this going on."

"Well, that's how I'm different. If you go to dinner with me, you're not going with a nice guy." He winked and then looked in the box. "No angel for the tree?"

Layla shook her head.

"This will have to be a cowboy tree." He pulled off his hat and placed it atop the tree, wrapping it with lights. "Perfect."

She had to agree. The tree was perfect.

She looked at Gage, with his perpetual five-o'clock shadow, his hair messy from the hat. Unfortunately for her heart, he was perfect, too.

Books by Brenda Minton

Love Inspired

Trusting Him
His Little Cowgirl
A Cowboy's Heart
The Cowboy Next Door
Rekindled Hearts
Blessings of the Season
  "The Christmas Letter"
Jenna's Cowboy Hero
The Cowboy's Courtship
The Cowboy's Sweetheart
Thanksgiving Groom
The Cowboy's Family
The Cowboy's Homecoming
Christmas Gifts
  *"Her Christmas Cowboy"

*The Cowboy's Holiday
  Blessing
*The Bull Rider's Baby
*The Rancher's Secret Wife
*The Cowboy's Healing Ways
*The Cowboy Lawman
  The Boss's Bride
*The Cowboy's Christmas
  Courtship

*Cooper Creek

BRENDA MINTON

started creating stories to entertain herself during hour-long rides on the school bus. In high school she wrote romance novels to entertain her friends. The dream grew and so did her aspirations to become an author. She started with notebooks, handwritten manuscripts and characters that refused to go away until their stories were told. Eventually she put away the pen and paper and got down to business with the computer. The journey took a few years, with some encouragement and rejection along the way—as well as a lot of stubbornness on her part. In 2006 her dream to write for Love Inspired Books came true. Brenda lives in the rural Ozarks with her husband, three kids and an abundance of cats and dogs. She enjoys a chaotic life that she wouldn't trade for anything—except, on occasion, a beach house in Texas. You can stop by and visit at her website, www.brendaminton.net.

The Cowboy's Christmas Courtship

Brenda Minton

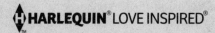

Recycling programs
for this product may
not exist in your area.

™ LOVE INSPIRED BOOKS

ISBN-13: 978-0-373-87843-7

THE COWBOY'S CHRISTMAS COURTSHIP

www.Harlequin.com

Printed in U.S.A.

For to us a child is born,
to us a son is given,
and the government will be on his shoulders.
And he will be called
Wonderful Counselor, Mighty God,
Everlasting Father, Prince of Peace.
—*Isaiah* 9:6

In memory of Ed Tonellato,
for all of his love and support.

Dedicated to Bonnie, Chloe and Lisa.

Chapter One

Gage Cooper hit a curve in the road going too fast. His truck slid a little, warning him to slow down. For the first time in a long time, he was in a hurry to get home. Maybe he wasn't ready to face the music or his well-meaning family, but at least home sounded good.

He thought maybe it was the time of year. It was the end of November, and with the holidays coming, winter edging in, it made Dawson, Oklahoma, inviting to a guy who had been on the road a lot. Maybe it was just time to make things right. When a guy looked death in the face, in the form of a one-ton bull, it made him think about how he'd treated the people in his life.

As if the bull hadn't been enough, Granny Myrna Cooper had called him last week to let him know what she thought of him. She'd said he was nearly twenty-seven, and he needed to figure out who he was and what he wanted.

What *did* he want to do with his life, other than ride bulls?

As the eleventh kid in the Cooper clan, that wasn't so easy a decision. Being second to the last sometimes made him feel like the kid waiting to get picked for a dodgeball team in grade school gym class. The kid that always got picked last. Or second to last.

He topped a hill, George Strait on the radio, his thoughts closing in on the homecoming that would take place in less than five minutes. Suddenly he saw a woman standing on the shoulder of the road as rain poured down. He hit the brakes. The truck slid sideways and came to a shuddering halt as a couple of rangy-looking cows and a calf walked across the paved country road.

The rain-soaked woman brushed hair from her face, and glared at him from where she stood in the ditch. A black-and-white border collie at her side hightailed it toward the cattle. He could ease the truck into first gear and pass on by once the cattle moved out of the road. His attention refocused on the woman standing in the ditch, tiny and pale, big work gloves on small hands.

No, he wasn't going to drive on by. He was a Cooper. Cooper men weren't bred to leave a woman in distress. Man, sometimes he wished they were. The woman standing in that ditch had a bucketful of reasons to dislike him. Good reasons, too.

He parked his truck, sighing as he grabbed his jacket and shoved the door open, easing down, careful not to land on his left leg. Rain poured down. It was the kind of rain that chilled a man to the bone.

The cows scattered. The dog nipped at hooves and the woman, Layla Silver, called a command. She held wire cutters. A big chunk of fence had been cut and the barbed wire pulled back. Why didn't she just run the cattle to the nearest gate?

Gage moved to block the cows from running down

the road. Layla ignored him, except to flash him a brief, irritated look. Well deserved. He'd been driving too fast for this road, in this weather.

She moved a little as the dog brought the cattle around.

"Nice driving," she eventually said.

Gage stood his ground, keeping the cows from slipping past his truck. When the cattle moved, he got in behind them, pushing them back to the ditch, in the direction of the fence. He didn't respond to Layla's criticism. He had it coming, and for a lot more than driving so fast.

A heifer tried to break free and turned to run past him.

"Watch that one," Layla shouted, her long brown hair soaked and rain dripping down her face.

He shook his head to clear his thoughts and moved, helping the dog bring the cow back to the herd. The animals moved through the soggy ditch. Gage eased his right leg first because the brace on his left knee didn't have a lot of give, not for stomping through grassy ditches or rounding up cattle.

He was two weeks postsurgery. Maybe he should explain that to Layla, not that she would care. She stood back as the cows and the calf went through the break in the fence and then she grabbed the barbed wire and started making repairs, twisting with pliers held in her gloved hands.

"Let me do that." He reached for the pliers and she looked up, gray eyes big in a pretty face, her mouth twisted into a frown.

"I can do it myself, thank you." She held tight and fixed the fence as he stood there like the jerk he was.

"Why'd you cut the fence?"

"It was cut by someone other than me. I finished it off so I could go ahead and put them back in, then fix it."

"Who…"

"If I knew that, I'd put a stop to it. You can go now."

Yeah, he could, but that would make him a bigger jerk than he'd been years ago. At seventeen he'd been pretty full of himself. A few months short of twenty-seven, he should be making things right. Another fact about a bull headed straight at a guy, it made him want to fix things. His life had flashed before his eyes. Every wrong thing he'd done, and there'd been a lot.

"I'll give you a ride to your place," he offered.

"I can walk."

"Layla, it's pouring and it's cold, just get in the truck."

She shoved the pliers into the pocket of her jacket and stared up at him. Somewhere along the way she'd gotten real pretty. Not made up, overly polished kind of pretty. She was naturally pretty with big gray eyes, sooty lashes and a sweet smile. When she smiled.

"I'll walk."

"No, you won't. Don't make me have to pick you up and put you in that truck."

"Stop pretending to be a nice guy, Gage Cooper." Her voice broke a little. She turned and started to walk away.

Her house was back down the road and then up her long drive, unless she walked through the field. The rain had gone from steady to a downpour. He reached for her arm, lifted her up off the ground and trudged through the ditch with her. She smacked his back, kicking him to get loose. Gage cringed, because this probably wasn't what his surgeon would call "taking it easy."

With what felt like a wildcat in his arms he climbed the slight incline to his truck, yanked the door open and deposited the soaking wet female on the seat. Man, this was exactly why he didn't play the nice guy. Because it didn't work for him. Women didn't fall over with soft eyes and smiles. They fought him, and in general thought he couldn't do a nice thing unless he was after something in return.

He whistled and told the dog to get in the back before he limped around the front of the truck and climbed in behind the wheel. Layla sat in the passenger seat, shivering. He turned up the heat, shifted into Drive and pulled back onto the road.

"Thank you for helping, Gage. I guess you're not such a bad guy." He mimicked a female voice and saw her lips turn just a little. He went a step further and forced his voice a little deeper than reality. "Why, you're welcome, Layla. And thank you for noticing."

He offered a flirty grin that usually worked. She didn't smile back. She wasn't the kind of woman he was used to.

"You're not a nice guy, but thank you for helping."

"Okay, you get the points for that one. I'm not a nice guy. Where's your brother?" Because the kid had to be a teenager now and old enough to help out.

"I'm not sure."

He let it go because the cool tone of her voice told him it wasn't any of his business. He would drop her off at her place and head on to Cooper Creek Ranch. End of story. Yep, none of his business.

But for some reason those thoughts pulled a long

sigh from deep down in his chest. It had a lot to do with that moment on the ground before the bull tried to trample the life out of him. It had to do with facing the past. His past. And now, his past with Layla.

Because Layla was probably the person he'd hurt the most. And then life had hurt her even more. Another reason he was angry with God, he guessed. Layla and Reese, two people who didn't deserve the rotten hands they'd been dealt. Why did good people suffer while Gage walked through life without a care in the world?

Layla closed her eyes for a brief moment to gather her wits and push back the sting of tears. She was so tired. So completely exhausted. She'd been tired for seven years and it wasn't getting any easier. Seven years ago her little brother, Brandon, had been eight years old, and he'd needed her. Now he needed someone with a firmer hand than hers. But she was all he had. They were the last of the Silvers.

Their parents had died in a car accident just months past her nineteenth birthday. Somehow she'd convinced a judge to give her custody of her little brother. Her plans for college, dating, getting married, had ended the day she and Brandon walked through the doors of their house. He had needed her.

The truck slowed, then bounced and bumped up the long driveway to her house. She opened her eyes as they drew close to the little white house she'd been raised in. Her stomach churned, thinking about how hard it had been lately to hold on to it.

She'd lost a decent job in Grove and replaced it with an okay job at the feed store in Dawson. She'd had to take out a loan against the place to put the new roof on last summer and then to pay for the medical bills when Brandon broke his arm.

"You okay?"

Gage's voice cut into her thoughts. Why'd he have to sound like he cared? Oh, that's right, because he was good at pretending. For a second she'd almost fallen for it. Again. And that made her feel sixteen and naive. The way she'd been when he'd sat down next to her at lunch one day back in high school. He'd offered her a piece of his mom's pie and then told her he needed help with chemistry.

"I'm good," she answered. She'd fallen in love with him her junior year. He'd walked her to class. He'd taken her to the Mad Cow Café; he'd been sweet.

He stopped the truck in front of her house and before she could protest, he walked around to her side to open the door. The last thing she wanted from him was chivalry. She didn't want or need his kindness.

"I said I'm good." She hopped down from the truck. "I didn't get my knee busted up in the world finals or get a concussion that knocked me out for a day."

"But I won." He grinned and she held her breath, because that handsome, cowboy grin with those hazel green eyes of his could do a number on any girl, even one who wasn't interested.

He was scruffy, and sorely needed a shave and a haircut, because his brown hair was shaggy. That made her smile a little, because she liked the thought of the homecoming he'd get looking like something the dog dragged in on the carpet. Ripped jeans, threadbare T-shirt beneath a denim jacket and several days behind in shaving. His mom, Angie Cooper, wouldn't be happy.

"I'm going inside," she announced.

He glanced away from her, to the stack of wood at the side of the house and then up, at the thin stream of smoke coming from the chimney. "I'll grab some wood."

"Please don't."

He turned and looked at her. The rain had slowed to a steady drizzle, but drops of moisture dripped from his hat. She swiped at her face and headed to the porch. "Go home."

"I'm going to get you a stack of wood and make you a pot of coffee."

"I drink tea."

"I'll make you a cup of tea."

She stomped up to him. "I don't want you to do this. Your guilt is the last thing I need."

"It isn't…" He shrugged off the denial. "I'm going to get you a load of wood in and make you a cup of tea while you get warm."

"I would rather you not. I can get my own firewood and make my own tea."

For a second she thought he might leave. He looked down at her, emotions flickering through his eyes. And then he smiled. "Layla, I'm sorry. It was a long time ago, and I haven't done much to make things right. Let me get the wood. Please."

Contrition. She always fell for it. Every time her little brother said he'd help more or do better, she believed him. Gage had soft eyes that almost convinced her he meant what he said. Besides, she was older now. She could withstand that Cooper charm.

"Okay." She inclined her head to the woodpile. "Thank you."

As he trudged off, grabbing a wheelbarrow along the way, she headed for the house. She'd managed to get a wreath on the front door and the other day she'd bought a pine-scented candle. That was as far as she'd gotten with Christmas cheer.

When she walked through the front door she shivered and wanted to keep her jacket on. But it was soaked through. She hung it on the coatrack by the door and did a quick search for her brother.

Brandon was nowhere to be seen. She thought maybe he'd taken off with friends while she'd been out in the barn. He was hard to keep hold of these days. And he was less help now than he'd been as a little boy.

She needed some warm clothes. The sound of wood thumping into a wheelbarrow meant Gage was still outside. She hurried upstairs to her room and pulled a warm sweatshirt over her T-shirt. Her hair was still wet so she ran a towel over her head, then dried her face. As she walked down the stairs, she heard clanking and banging from the living room. Wood smoke filled the air and she smiled.

Gage Cooper squatted in front of her cantankerous old fireplace insert, rattling the vents and coughing as smoke filled the room. She hurried forward and twisted the right lever. The smoke started up the chimney again. He looked up at her.

"Sorry, I couldn't get it to work."

She shrugged off the apology. "It takes skill."

"I have skill."

"Of course you do." She glanced at the pile of wood on the hearth. "Thank you for bringing that in. I could make you a cup of coffee but I don't have a coffeemaker. I only drink tea."

"I'm good." He shoved in another log. The embers glowed brighter, sparked, and the fire came back to life. "There you go."

He pushed himself to his feet. Layla's hand went out to steady him, but she pulled back, unwilling to make contact. He smiled at her, as if he knew.

"I'll make tea." She walked away, leaving him to make the slow trail after her. "And then you should go."

She called back the last without looking at him.

He chuckled in response.

When he entered the kitchen she turned, watching as he sat at the rickety old table that had been in the house since before her birth. The wood had faded. The chairs wobbled. She'd tightened them dozens of times over the years but they were close to being firewood.

"So, how's…"

She cut him off. "Let's not make small talk and pretend to be friends."

The microwave beeped and she pulled out a cup of hot water, dropping a tea bag in before chastising herself for sounding like a shrew. But the stern lecture didn't last long. He deserved her anger.

She looked at him as she dunked the tea bag. He had settled on one of those wobbly chairs, his left leg straight in front of him. His hat was on the table and he'd folded his arms over his chest.

"I'm sorry that I hurt you."

"I think you've said that before." She put the second cup of water in the microwave and brought the finished cup of tea to Gage.

"I was a kid, Layla. I was spoiled and thought I could do no wrong. I didn't think about your feelings."

The words stunned her because he sounded so amazingly sincere. His face looked sincere. His eyes looked sincere. She was not a good judge of character. She was the person who kicked the dog out of the house for chewing up shoes and then let him back in, thinking he wouldn't do it again.

The few relationships she'd had in her teen years had been with the wild ones her mother had warned her to stay away from. But then, at sixteen her mom had told her to fall in love with a Cooper, a man who would treat her right.

Layla didn't want to think of all the reasons her mom had said that to her. The list had been long. Her mom's life had been hard. She hadn't wanted her daughter to follow in her footsteps. Layla's mom had wanted her to marry someone who would take care of her, who wouldn't hurt her.

"Layla, I mean it. I'm sorry."

"Right, I know. I'm no longer a naive kid, so thank you for the life lesson and now for the apology but…"

He grinned again. "But you'd rather hold the past over my head."

I'd rather keep my heart safe. "I'd rather you drink your tea and go."

Because if he sat there any longer, she'd remember how it felt when they studied chemistry together, and how she'd discovered chemistry of a different kind when he kissed her, a sweetly chaste kiss but one that had changed her life. And then she learned that he'd been using her to get to her best friend. At sixteen, it had felt like the worst thing that could ever happen. If only she'd known how much more life could hurt, she would have cried less over him.

As for her best friend, Cheryl, the friendship had

ended. Not because of Gage, but because Cheryl had stayed in college when Layla had come home to raise Brandon. Cheryl married a man from Texas, and she had a baby now.

From outside she could hear the loud engine of a truck. She heard laughter and then doors slamming. Brandon was home. After a few minutes he tumbled into the kitchen, bringing cold air and the strong odor of alcohol.

"What's for supper, sis?" He glanced in Gage's direction, grinned and plopped into a chair that nearly collapsed. "What's he doing here? Got yourself a new man? One with money?"

Before she could stop him, Gage Cooper jumped out of his chair. He grabbed her little brother by the front of his shirt and pulled him to his feet. Gage's face went red and Brandon's went a few shades paler.

"Don't talk to your sister that way."

"Or you'll what?" Brandon slurred. "What'll you do, Gage Cooper?"

"I'll mop the floor with your sorry hide."

"Oh, right, because you always do the right thing."

Gage let him drop into his chair. Layla hurried to separate the two of them.

"Gage, you should go."

Gage looked long at her brother and then at her. "Layla, you deserve more respect than that. More than either of us has shown you."

"He's a kid. He's made mistakes."

"He needs someone to yank a knot in his tail."

"It won't be you. He's my brother and we're handling things."

"Of course you are." He looked around and she knew

that he was seeing the ramshackle house for what it was. The kitchen appliances were on their last legs. The floors were sagging in spots. Insulation was nonexistent. Wind blew in through the windows strong enough to move the curtains.

"We are." But she was barely holding it together at the moment. She knew how to be strong. But she didn't know how to accept his sympathy.

Gage leaned over Brandon again. "If I ever hear you talk to your sister like that again, you'll answer to me."

"Whatever." Her brother turned his head.

Gage let out a long sigh and pushed his cup in front of Brandon. "I'll take a rain check on the tea."

Layla nodded, too stunned to find the right words. She watched Gage shove his hat back on his head and walk slowly down the hall to the front door. A minute later his truck started, and she knew he was gone.

The fight left her in one fell swoop. She sat down at the table and reached for the steaming cup of green tea. Brandon leaned forward and lost his lunch all over the kitchen floor.

She was handling things.

She was handling being a single parent to a rebellious teenager. She was handling the bills that had to be paid. And somehow she would handle Gage Cooper being back in town.

Chapter Two

Gage rolled up the drive to Cooper Creek. He breathed in and out slowly, trying to let go of the urge to go back and beat some sense into Brandon Silver. But that would put him smack-dab in the middle of Layla's life, and that obviously wasn't where he wanted to be. Layla was the kind of woman a man married. He made a habit of staying away from the marrying kind.

He parked next to his brother Jackson's truck and got out. For a minute he stood in the driveway looking up at the big old house where he'd grown up. In a week it would be hung with lights and trimmed with red bows. His mom sure loved Christmas. And she loved her family.

He took off his hat and scratched his head. He didn't know why that love had been feeling like a noose for the past year or so. Maybe because it had felt like he couldn't meet any of the expectations placed on him. As he walked up the steps, the front door opened. His mom stood in the doorway, her smile huge. She wasn't a big lady but sometimes she seemed like a giant. She had a way of being strong and in control, even with a bunch of men in the family towering over her.

"It's about time." She smiled, and he smiled back.

"I haven't been gone that long."

"Since summer." She grabbed him in a big hug. "I thought you'd be here an hour ago. I was starting to worry. I even called your cell phone."

"I left it in my truck."

"Weren't you in your truck?" She pulled him inside. "Where were you?"

"Helping Layla Silver put some cattle in."

His mom's smile dissolved. "She's had a rough time of it lately. Word around town is that Brandon has been pulling some capers."

Capers. That was his mom's way of saying the kid was in deep trouble.

"What kind of capers?"

"Stealing, setting hay on fire and vandalizing. But he hasn't been caught, so it's all just hearsay."

"Well, right now he's sitting in her kitchen drunk."

"I've heard that, too. And it's a shame. His daddy was a horrible alcoholic before that accident. They say he was drunk that night."

"I know." He didn't need to hear the story again. He didn't need to relive his own guilt again. "What's for dinner?"

Change of subject. His mom looked up at him, her smile fading into a frown. "I thought we were discussing Layla?"

"I know what we were doing. Now we're avoiding discussing Layla."

He'd like to avoid reliving his past and all of his mistakes in the first few hours of returning home. There wasn't a thing he could do about what he'd done. He couldn't do anything about the injustices in the world, when guys like him walked through life without a bump or bruise while the good guys took the hits.

Good guys, like his brother Reese, blinded after an explosion in Afghanistan. Gage was not on good terms with God right now, and Reese was the big reason why.

The last thing he wanted to think about was Layla, and how he'd become her friend because Cheryl Gayle wouldn't talk to him. Finally, after a few short dates with Cheryl, he'd realized his mistake. She'd been pretty—and pretty close to annoying.

And he'd missed Layla. He always thought she'd be married by now. If things had been different, she probably would have been.

"Gage, I'm glad you're home," Angie Cooper said, reading the look on his face.

"I'm glad I'm home, too." He walked with her through the big living room. In a few days they'd put up a tree. Not a real one. They'd changed to fake trees the year his brother Travis met Elizabeth. Her allergies had almost done her in that first Christmas.

Now the wagon ride they used to take to cut down a tree was just a wagon ride. They would all pile in the two wagons, take a ride through the field and then come home to hot cocoa and cookies. Family traditions. The Coopers did love them.

He wasn't crazy about them. He'd been living in Oklahoma City off and on. Had even spent some time down in Texas. Anything to avoid coming home.

"It was good to have Dad out there for the last night of the finals." It had been even better to wake up in the hospital and see his dad sitting next to the bed.

"He was thrilled that he could be there. And so proud of you. But I would have liked for you to come home and have the surgery here instead of in Texas." His mom touched his arm. "How is Dylan?"

Dylan was a year older than Gage, and the two brothers had always been close. Dylan had been living in Texas for about a year, avoiding the family. Mainly because he had known they wouldn't understand what he was doing. "Mom, he'll be home as soon as he can."

"Why is he doing this?"

"Because Casey is his friend, and she needs someone to help her while she goes through chemo. She doesn't have family."

"I know but it's a big responsibility for a young man."

"He's twenty-eight, and you've taught us all to help those in need."

"It's one lesson you've all learned." She hooked her arm through his. "Jackson is here."

"Good. I meant to tell him about a few bulls that are going up for sale."

"You boys and those bucking bulls." She shook her head. He didn't mind that she didn't get it. She got just about everything else that mattered. Before she walked away he hugged her again.

"I've missed you."

She smiled at that, "I've missed you, too. Sometimes I don't know if you know how much. Which reminds me. You missed Thanksgiving last Thursday. But you did not miss serving dinner tonight at the Back Street Community Center."

He nearly groaned. He hadn't timed this as well as

he'd thought. Each year they had a community dinner a week after Thanksgiving.

"How long do I have?"

She patted his back. "A few hours. Don't try to leave."

From the kitchen he heard Jackson laugh. Gage walked into the big open room that always smelled like something good was cooking, and usually was. He ignored Jackson and opened the oven door. Rolls. He inhaled the aroma and closed the door.

"Better stay out of there or Mom will have your hide." Jackson poured himself a cup of coffee and offered one to Gage.

"No, thanks."

"Did I hear you say something about Layla Silver?"

Gage shook his head.

Jackson took a sip of coffee and stared at him over the rim of the cup. Gage zeroed in on the pies lined up on the counter. He went for one but his mom slapped his hand away.

"Those are for the community center."

"I had restaurant food for Thanksgiving. Don't I rate at least a piece of pumpkin pie?"

"Not on your life, cowboy. You could have come home."

"I couldn't leave Dylan."

His mom went to the fridge and opened the door. "I have a coconut cream pie I made a couple of days ago. Knock yourself out."

"Thanks, Mom. That's why you're the best. Where's Dad?"

"He took a load of cattle to Tulsa. He's staying there tonight."

Gage grabbed a fork and headed for the table to fin-ish off the pie. "So, you guys have fun at the commu-nity center."

He knew he wouldn't get away with skating out on helping. He thought it would be fun to try. He took a bite of pie, closing his eyes just briefly to savor the taste. His mom's pies were the best.

"You're going with me," his mom said from the kitchen as she opened the oven door and removed the homemade rolls. "Jackson, Madeline and Jade are help-ing, too."

"You know I can't stand for long periods of time." He grinned as he tried out his last excuse, pointing to the knee he'd had surgery on.

"We'll get you a chair to sit on."

He'd lost. He knew when to let it go.

Jackson sat down next to him. "Lucky for you, Layla Silver will be there, too."

"Thanks...that makes it all better." Gage finished off his pie. "I'm going to get cleaned up."

He made it upstairs to his room and collapsed on the bed that had the same bedspread he'd used as a teen. The posters on the walls were of bull riders he'd looked up to as a kid. Justin McBride, J. W. Hart and Chris Shivers. He crooked one arm behind his head and thought about how life had changed. He'd wanted to be them. Now he rode in some of the same events they'd ridden in. But he was still running from life.

Since he had time he flipped on the TV and searched for reruns of the finals. He didn't find them so he set-tled for a few minutes of a popular sitcom. A guy who had made mistakes and was trying to make amends to the people he'd hurt. Gage thought about how much he had in common with the guy in that show. Since his bull wreck at the finals, he'd been thinking a lot about his list of wrongs.

How did he make amends to the people he'd hurt? Where did he start? He sighed, because he knew that he needed to start with the person he'd hurt the most. The person who liked him the least.

How did he do that without giving her the wrong idea?

The parking lot at Back Street Community Center held about fifty cars. So far there were only a dozen or so. Layla parked her old truck and reached for the green bean casserole she'd brought. In the passenger seat, Brandon looked miserable and almost as green as the casserole.

"Come on. You can help serve." She handed him the dish. "Don't drop it."

"I think I can manage to carry a pan." He had that sullen, teen look on his face. She ignored it because she knew he wanted to get a rise out of her.

"Let's go, then."

"Why can't I help the guys put together the buildings for the nativity?" He nodded in the direction of Bethlehem, or at least the Dawson version.

As they walked by, the star over the manger lit up briefly, flickered and went out again. Someone yelled that they'd found the short in the cord.

Brandon slowed, probably hoping she'd tell him to do what he wanted. She shook her head.

"You're going inside."

He groaned. "I thought helping out was a good thing, and you're telling me I can't."

"You're helping, just not where you want to help."

They walked through the light mist to the front of the church that Jeremy and Beth Hightree had turned into a community center. Brandon lagged, his face one of absolute misery. For a second she almost caved, nearly told him he could help with the nativity buildings. But then she remembered why she'd dragged him along.

Days like this made her wish for someone to lean on. An aunt or uncle, anyone. But the one uncle they had was just as bad an alcoholic as their father had been. An aunt who was married lived in Africa. She and her husband were missionaries and rarely came home.

She walked through the doors of the old church and paused for a moment, feeling a wonderful sense of calm. The sanctuary of the church had been turned into a dining room. Tables were spread with white cloths. Pretty centerpieces added color. Layla could smell the aroma seeping up the steps. Turkey, ham, all of the typical Thanksgiving foods for this community dinner.

Peace. She looked to the front of the church where the wooden cross still hung on the wall. For a brief moment she closed her eyes and drew on a strength that came from within. She didn't have family to turn to but she had God. She had a community that loved her.

"Are you going to stand here all night?" Brandon sulked behind her.

"No." She moved on, walking through the sanctuary to the stairs.

"I'm going to stay the night with Lance," Brandon informed her as they headed down the stairs.

"No, you're not." She took the dish from his hands. The friend he'd mentioned was off-limits. "You're going to help me and then we're going home. And you're going to stay home. You're grounded."

"Layla, you're five feet tall. How are you gonna make me?" He towered over her. She knew he had a point. And it made her mad. In the past year he'd started challenging her, making things difficult. It had been easy when he was little. Now he needed a dad.

Standing in the kitchen of the community center, they had an audience. He did that on purpose. He picked public places to argue because he thought she would give in.

"Brandon, you're staying home."

"Who's going to stop me if I decide to leave?"

"I guess I'll make you." She knew that voice.

Gage stepped out of the shadows. He'd shaved and changed into new jeans and a button-up shirt. He'd left behind the shadow of growth on his chin. The dark stubble distracted her. He was talking again and Brandon looked a little cornered.

"Brandon, if I have to, I'll drive you home and I'll make sure you stay there."

Brandon smirked. "Who gave you a suit of armor and a white horse?"

Layla's thoughts exactly. Brandon had probably heard her say that at some point. She'd repeated more than once that she didn't need help. She could handle things. But lately it had been getting a lot harder. Losing her job had been the last straw.

"I don't need a suit of armor, jack…" Gage closed his mouth and then smiled across the kitchen at his mother, who had cleared her throat to stop him from going too far.

"Well, I don't need you to play daddy to me. I'm doing just fine."

Gage got close to her brother. "You're going to serve turkey, smile and be polite to your sister. If not, we'll call the police and have a talk with them about you coming home drunk."

Layla wanted to scream. Gage Cooper had been home for one day and suddenly he thought he had to ride to her rescue. She could do this. She'd been doing this for a long time. Her eyes filled with tears as she thought about how to take control of the situation.

Angie Cooper appeared at her side, always warm and smiling, always generous. Layla wanted to sink into her arms, but she couldn't let herself be comforted right now. It was too risky because she was too close to falling apart.

"Let Gage do this." Angie slipped an arm around Layla. "You need to take a deep breath and let people help."

Layla nodded, but she couldn't speak. Her strength was a thin cord that was unraveling. Instead of objections she mumbled something like "thank you," and then she allowed Angie Cooper to lead her back to the kitchen, where they searched for serving spoons and talked about the weather forecast.

People were starting to file in. There were families who might not have had a Thanksgiving dinner and people from the community who wanted fellowship with neighbors, talk about the price of cattle and the drought, maybe catch up on other news.

All around her, people were talking, smiling and laughing. Layla was trying to find a way to hold her life together and keep her brother from ruining his.

She served her green bean casserole and kept an eye on Brandon, who had been given the job of serving drinks.

She avoided looking at Gage. He'd found a kitchen stool to sit on while he served potatoes. From time to time he'd stand and stretch. Typical bull rider with a broken body and too much confidence.

Once, he caught her staring. He winked and she knew she turned a few shades of red. She could feel the heat crawl from her neck to her face, and probably straight to her hairline. She turned back to the next person in line and served a spoonful of green beans, smiling as if everything was perfect. Wonderful.

But Gage Cooper smiling at her was anything but perfect.

When the meal ended and the kitchen was clean, Layla went in search of her brother. She found him upstairs helping Gage carry bags of trash to the Dumpster. The night was dark and cold. The stars were hidden by clouds and the weatherman had said something about snow flurries. It was early in the season for snow in Oklahoma.

"Time to go." She stood on the sidewalk as they tossed the bags into the receptacle.

Gage turned to Brandon. "Get in my truck."

"Gage, I can do this." Layla pulled her jacket tight against the wind and looked from him to her brother.

"I know that." Gage pointed to his truck, and Brandon hurried across the parking lot like an eager puppy. Layla felt the first bits of anger coming to life.

"What in the world?" She watched Brandon climb in the passenger's side of Gage's truck.

"He's going to help me at the ranch tomorrow."

"Why?"

"To keep him out of trouble." Gage tilted his hat back and walked toward her. "Layla, I'm trying to help. Maybe show you that I'm sorry."

"So this is your way of making things right? You pretended to need help in chemistry."

"I did need help in chemistry." He grinned that Cooper grin that went straight to a girl's heart. Not hers, though. She knew better.

"And now I'm just a charity case that makes you feel better about yourself?"

"You aren't charity," he started. "But you're right. I am trying to feel better about myself."

"Use someone else to soothe your guilty conscience."

He smiled again, and her heart ached. "There are plenty of people that I need to make amends to. I'll get to them."

"As soon as you're done with me?" She shook her head. "At least you're honest."

"Yeah, trying to be." His eyes softened, hazel-green and fringed with dark lashes. "You're too good for me, Layla."

She thought about it for a minute. "You're right. I am too good for you."

"Exactly. Now, if you don't mind, I'm about done in. I'm going to drive your brother home, and I'll pick him up bright and early tomorrow morning."

"I have to work at the feed store in the morning. You might have to wake him up."

"I can do that. And I'll bring him home when you get off work."

She bit down on her bottom lip and stared up at him, wondering if this was another game he was playing, a game she didn't have the rules for. He liked those games. She didn't. At the same time, she really needed help with her brother. Hadn't she whispered that prayer just hours earlier?

Across the way lights came on in Jeremy and Beth Hightree's home. The tree in the front window lit up, and a spotlight hit the manger in the yard. Christmas. It was a beautiful, wonderful time of hope and promise.

"I'm not sure." She looked from the Hightree's decorated house back to Gage.

"Layla, let me do this. The kid's in trouble and you need help with him."

She didn't want to admit it, but she did need help. She was worried about Brandon, about the guys he was hanging out with and the rumors about what they were doing. It had never been easy for her to accept help.

The first few years she'd worried that if she struggled, they'd take her brother away. It became a habit, doing things on her own.

"You can trust me."

She nodded and walked away, Gage's words following her to her truck. She doubted that she could trust him, but for a few minutes she had the very break she'd been praying for.

She would have to accept that it had been given to her by Gage Cooper. He was home, and she would have to face the past, and the way he'd hurt her all those years ago.

Chapter Three

Gage pulled up to the Silver place the next morning. It was eight o'clock and he'd already been to the barn that morning. He'd fed horses, driven out to check on cattle grazing on the back part of the ranch and then he'd had a big breakfast. Jackson had showed up to work with some young bulls they were hoping to buck next spring.

He walked up to the square white house, just a box with wood siding, a fairly new metal roof and a front porch that could use a few new boards. The only sign of Christmas was the wreath on the front door. He guessed it was still early, barely December.

The house was silent. Gage knocked on the door twice. No one answered. He turned the doorknob. It was unlocked so he walked inside and walked from room to room. No sign of Brandon. He went back outside. Maybe the kid had actually gotten up early to feed for Layla. But Gage doubted it.

He walked out to the barn, his left leg stiff in the brace. It was going to be a long two months gimping around. The dog joined him. It wagged its tail, rolled over on its back for him to rub its belly. He obliged and then straightened to look around.

The few head of cattle were munching hay. He turned, scanning the horizon. That's when he spotted a lone figure heading across the field in the direction of town.

"Good grief." He shook his head and turned back to the truck. The dog followed. "Stay."

The border collie sat, tail wagging, brushing dirt back and forth. He smiled at the dog. "Okay, you can go."

The dog ran to his truck and jumped in the back. He doubted Layla would thank him for that. He'd call her later and let her know where the animal had gone. As he pulled down the drive he watched the figure getting smaller and smaller. Brandon had cut through the field and he was climbing the fence to get to the road. Gage hit the gas and took off, dust and gravel flying out behind his truck.

When he pulled up next to the kid, Brandon shot him a dirty look and kept walking. Gage rolled down his window.

"Get in."

"I can't. I told a friend I'd help him get some hay up today."

"There isn't anyone putting up hay at the end of November." Gage stopped the truck. "Get in, now. If you don't, I'll call the police and we'll see what they think about underage drinking."

"Like you've never done it." Brandon stopped. He stood at the side of the road, all anger and teenage rebellion.

"Right, well, I've done a lot I'm not proud of. But I never came home and puked on my mom's floor."

"She's my sister, not my mom." Brandon shot him a look and then looked back at the road ahead of him. "How'd you know?"

"I overheard Layla telling someone at the dinner last night. You know, she's given up just about everything to stay home and take care of you. The least you could do is man up a little and help her out. She only got one semester of college in before she had to be a full-time mom to you. I don't think she's had much of a social life. She sure isn't having a lot of fun."

Brandon walked toward the truck. "Aren't you the user who pretended you liked her back in high school?"

"I told you, I've done a lot I'm not proud of."

"So now you get to tell me how to live? Maybe we could both get right with Jesus on Sunday."

Gage whistled low. "You don't really play fair."

"No, I don't. I just figure you aren't really the best guy to be preaching at me."

Gage opened his truck door fast, and Brandon jumped back, no longer grinning. "Get in the truck."

Brandon's hands went up in surrender, and he put distance between himself and Gage by walking around the truck to get in on the passenger side. Gage climbed back behind the wheel and shifted into gear. Neither of them talked for a while. As they were pulling up the drive of Cooper Creek Ranch, Brandon glanced in the back of the truck.

"Is that my dog?"

Gage pulled up to the barn. "Yeah, I guess it is."

"What's she doing here?"

"She acted like she didn't want to be left at home alone today."

"That's crazy. Layla's going to be pretty ticked if she comes home and the dog is gone."

"I'll call and tell her I have you and the dog." He parked and got out of the truck. Brandon took his time joining him.

The side door of the barn opened, and Jackson walked out, his hat pulled low. He took off leather gloves and looked from Gage to Brandon before shaking his head. He shoved the gloves in his jacket pocket and waited.

"You two ready to work?" Jackson made strong eye contact with Brandon.

"Sure, why not." Brandon edged past Jackson into the barn.

"Nice kid." Jackson slapped Gage on the back. "The two of you can be surly together."

"I'm not surly." Gage strode past his brother, not much different from what Brandon had done. He watched him walk down the aisle between stalls, looking closely at the horses in the stalls.

"Nice horses." Brandon stopped in front of the stall that belonged to the champion quarter horse Jackson and Lucky had bought a year or so back.

"Yeah, he's nice all right. Don't let Jackson catch you messing around with him."

"Yeah, guess we could actually pay off the mortgage on the farm and then some with a horse like that."

Mortgage. Gage tried to pretend he hadn't heard the remark, but it settled in his mind, making him wonder what mortgage they could have on a nearly decrepit farmhouse and twenty acres of rough land.

Maybe that explained the dark circles under Layla's eyes? Not that a guy was supposed to notice those things. He'd learned that lesson from his sisters the hard way.

"Where do we start?" Brandon moved on past the stallion to the office.

Gage followed him inside and watched as the teen took a seat and kicked back, his booted feet on the desk.

"Get your feet down." Gage knocked Brandon's feet off the desk. "First, we have steers needing to be vaccinated. We'll drive them into a round pen on the twenty where they're pastured."

"Fine. Let's go."

Gage motioned him toward the door. The two of them headed for an old farm truck. Jackson was stowing supplies in the metal toolbox on the back of the truck. He turned as they approached.

"Ready to go?"

"We're ready," Gage opened the door and motioned Brandon in. He joined Jackson at the back of the truck. "Is there anything you need me to grab?"

"Nope, I have lunch in the cooler and coffee in the thermos. We're set to go."

"Let's do it then."

"Gage, why are you doing this?"

"Doing what?"

Jackson shot a look at the cab of the truck where Brandon waited, and then back to Gage. "Don't play stupid."

"I'm helping Layla get control of her little brother before he lands himself in trouble."

"Out of the goodness of your heart?"

"Yeah, why not?" Gage started to walk away but Jackson stopped him.

"When do you ever do anything just because it helps someone else?"

Anger flared but quickly evaporated because Jackson had a point. "So, I haven't been the most charitable Cooper ever. But sometimes a guy sees the right thing to do and he does it."

"And it has nothing to do with Layla Silver being downright pretty and available?"

"Layla's pretty?" He scrunched his eyebrows in thought and scratched his chin. "Yeah, I guess she is."

"She's also the girl you treated poorly back in high school."

"Well, maybe I've decided to make a few things right." He was itching to get away from Jackson and this conversation, but Jackson didn't appear to be letting go any more than a dog that had found a good bone.

"Making amends, are we?" Jackson headed for the driver's side door of the truck.

"Yeah, something like that."

"There's a lot more to it than just doing a few good deeds to make you feel better."

Gage whistled for Layla's dog and pointed to the back of the truck. Once the animal was in, he walked around the truck to climb in. He wished he could get in his truck and take off, no looking back.

But he'd made a commitment, and he was going to see it through. Besides, even though he didn't want to admit it, he didn't feel like running.

After work that evening, Layla drove up to Cooper Creek Ranch to get her little brother. She parked her old truck in front of the two-story garage, but she didn't get out right away. It felt too good to sit in the truck and relax. The silence felt almost as good as the sitting.

A scratching on the door of her truck caught her attention. She pushed the door open and Daisy jumped back, wagging her feathery black tail and panting ninety-to-nothing.

"Traitor," she said. Daisy didn't mind. Instead she licked Layla's hand and then ran off in the direction of the barn.

Layla started walking in the direction the dog had gone, her feet dragging. The barn made her poor old wood building look miserable by comparison. Her barn had been built by her grandfather in the early 1900s. This barn was a metal building, half stable and half arena. It even had an apartment attached.

The Coopers had a little of everything. Quarter horses, bucking bulls, cattle, not to mention the banks, oil and apartment complexes. They were wealthy, but they were also the kindest people she knew. They were generous and good to their neighbors. Not that they were without their own problems. Not that their children, most now grown, didn't occasionally do something wrong. She guessed she liked the Coopers because they were genuine and sometimes they messed up.

She walked to the barn but she didn't go in. Early evening had settled over the countryside, turning the sky dusky gray and pink. In the field cattle grazed. It was peaceful. She needed that moment of peace. It was too cold to stay outside, though, and she'd left her jacket in the truck. She shivered, reaching for the door as it opened. She jumped out of the way.

Jackson Cooper smiled as he stepped through the door. "Layla, long day?"

"Always." Every day for nearly eight years. She managed a smile. "Is Brandon making a nuisance of himself?"

"Not at all. We worked him hard today. He asked about pay and Gage said we're putting part of it in an account for college and giving the rest to you to decide what he gets."

"Really? That was Gage's plan?"

Jackson grinned. "He came home responsible or guilty. Whatever happened, he's trying to help you out."

"He doesn't owe me."

"He thinks he does."

"I should get Brandon and go. I'm sure you all have more to do than keeping my brother out of trouble."

"Go on in. They're in the arena. I'm heading home." Jackson patted her shoulder and walked away as she headed into the barn.

She could hear them in the arena. Her steps slowed as she neared the entrance that led from the stable to the arena. She listened carefully to the clank of metal, the pounding of hooves, shouts from someone other than Gage or Brandon.

Through the wide opening in the arena she saw her brother in a metal chute, settling on the back of a bull.

She yelled out, "No!" But it was too late. The gate opened and the bull came spinning out, her brother clamped down tight on its back. She walked fast around the metal enclosure, keeping a cautious eye on the bull and her brother.

The ride didn't last long. The bull spun fast and Brandon went flying. He rolled out of the way as

Travis Cooper moved between him and the animal. Gage headed her way, grinning, obviously proud of himself. Quickly, something obviously clued him in to the fact that she was as far from happy as a woman could get. His smile faded and he shot a worried glance in the direction of the arena, where her brother had gotten to his feet.

"How dare you!" She pushed past him to open the gate now that the bull had been penned up. "Brandon, let's go. We're going home."

"I'm not." Brandon said, but then he had the sense to look a little worried.

"I didn't give you permission to ride bulls. I don't have the money for hospital bills. And I can't…" She couldn't lose anyone else. She swallowed the lump that lodged in her throat and refused to look at Gage. He had a hand on her arm but she shook her head. She didn't want to see sympathy in his eyes.

She avoided those looks from people. Had made it a habit right after her parents died. Those looks had turned her into a sobbing mess, and she'd had to be strong. She didn't have time to fall apart. Brandon needed her to be strong.

"It was a steer," Gage offered. "I wouldn't let him get hurt. And I'm not going to start him out on our bulls. Come on, Layla, you know that."

"Right." She motioned Brandon through the gate. "We're going home. I have chores to do and I still have to cook dinner."

"I ate with the Coopers, and we did the chores at the house a couple hours ago." Brandon kept his eyes down, staring at his boots.

"Thank you." The anger seeped out, leaving her

shaking and weak. "But I haven't eaten and I'm ready to go home."

"Layla, can we talk?" Gage maneuvered her away from Brandon and Travis. "We'll catch up with you guys at the house."

"Right." Travis gave Gage a long look before nodding. "Come on, Brandon, we'll see if there's any leftover pie."

Travis and her brother walked out of the arena, leaving her alone with Gage. He nodded toward the bleachers that served as seating when the Coopers held small events on the ranch. Layla didn't want to sit and talk. She wanted to go home and put her feet up. Most of all she wanted *not* to think about Gage Cooper or how her life was falling apart while he played at fixing his.

She sat down on the second row of seating, shivering as the cool metal bench seeped into her bones, chilling her. Gage didn't sit down. He shrugged out of his canvas jacket and placed it around her shoulders.

"Thank you." She looked up at him, wishing he could always be this person. But this Gage was the dangerous Gage. He was the person a girl could lose her heart to. Even when she knew better.

"Let me teach him to ride bulls."

Gage gave her an easy smile. Life was a big adventure for him. He traveled. He rode bulls. He lived for himself. She closed her eyes because she knew she wasn't being fair.

When she opened her eyes, he was watching her. Intent. Curious. Handsome in a way that made a girl's heart melt. It was his eyes, she thought, and shook her head.

"I do not want him to ride bulls, Gage. I want him

to grow up, go to college, get married and have kids. I want…"

She couldn't say that she wanted him to be grown-up so she could stop worrying. That wasn't fair. She'd known when their parents died that her life had to be put on hold to raise her brother. She had worked hard to keep the authorities from placing him with strangers.

She'd put aside her dreams of college, a career, marriage and children. That wasn't Brandon's fault.

"I'll keep him on steers until I know he can handle bulls. I think if you'll listen to me, you'll understand why this is important."

She looked up, meeting those sincere hazel eyes of his. He'd been in the Southwest, so his skin was still golden-brown from the sun. "Tell me."

"He needs something to keep him busy and people who will keep him busy. He's in with a bad crowd right now, Layla. You can't be with him all of the time. So if he's here when he isn't at school, we can keep him out of trouble. I can help you with that."

"Right, so this is about you?"

He grinned again, white teeth flashing. "Could you stop being so mean?"

Layla closed her eyes and nodded. "I'm sorry. I'm not a mean person. I'm just tired."

The bleachers moved and creaked as he sat down next to her. His shoulder bumped hers, and she inhaled the scent of the outdoors. How could he smell that good when he'd been working all day?

"I know you're not mean." His voice was soft. "I was teasing."

Her heart tried to open up. She couldn't let it. "You hurt me."

"I know and I'm sorry."

She nodded, not looking at him because she couldn't look into his eyes right then, not when her emotions were worn thin and she needed someone to lean on. It couldn't be him.

"What is it you're doing, Gage? Are you trying to earn my forgiveness?"

"I don't know." He leaned back against the bleacher seat behind them and stretched his leg in front of him. "Maybe I'm trying to find my way back."

"God doesn't require you to make amends to be forgiven."

He didn't respond for a minute. She wondered if she'd hit the nail on the head. She looked up at him. He was staring at the arena, his strong jaw clenched. She focused, for whatever reason, on the pulse at the base of his throat.

Finally he sighed. "I have to do this."

"I forgave you a long time ago. When we're young everything feels like forever. I was a typical teenage girl who thought if you smiled at me, we'd probably get married. I know better now."

"Girls really think that?" He smiled at her.

"Maybe not that drastically. But when the teenage girl is already…" She didn't want to have this conversation, but it was too late. "When the girl isn't feeling loved, she is probably looking for someone to love her."

"I'm sorry that I wasn't the person to love you."

So was she. "Well, you did me a favor. You taught me to be more careful. We've all hurt people, Gage. It's part of life, part of growing up."

"I know. But somehow I've skated through life with

almost no repercussions and other people have suffered…."

He had more to say, but she didn't want to hear it. They weren't friends. They didn't share secrets. She stood up and moved away from him, away from his story and his emotions.

"I should go."

He grinned and stood up. "Too much?"

"Yeah. I think if you need to confess, I'm not the person. But I'll take the help with my brother."

"Thank you."

She took off his coat and handed it back to him. His fingers brushed hers. Layla pulled back, surprised by the contact, by the way his eyes sought hers when they touched.

"Good night, Gage." She hurried away, leaving him standing in the arena alone.

Chapter Four

Gage didn't plan on going to church with the family Sunday morning, so he woke up before sunrise and headed out, dressed for work in old jeans, a flannel shirt and work boots. Layla had a few fences that looked like a cow could walk right through them, and he knew she'd fight him if he offered. So he wasn't going to ask, he was just going to do it.

It was cold, so cold he could see his breath as he walked along the fence line after parking his truck at the end of Layla's drive. Talk about a mess. The fence posts leaned and the barbed wire was so loose a cow could walk between the strands.

He didn't know why kids had bothered cutting the fence. They could have pushed the fence posts over. But not after today. He planned on pounding the posts back into the ground and tightening the wire, maybe replacing some of it.

It would take all day. So he wouldn't have to sit across the Sunday table from Reese and fight his anger all over again. He wasn't angry with Reese, but with the hand he'd been dealt. Gage wouldn't have to go to church and face God with that anger.

He stopped at the corner post. The sun was coming up over the tree line, shooting beams of light into the hazy morning. It wouldn't take long for it to burn up the fog and melt the frost that covered the grass and trees. But it sure was beautiful.

As the sun rose, he pounded away at fence posts, working his way down the line. He eventually had to get his sunglasses, and then went back to work. He didn't know how Layla did it all. She was working, trying to keep her brother from becoming a juvenile delinquent and holding on to this farm. He shot a look toward the house, a good thousand feet to the east of where he stood. At that moment she walked out the back door, her tiny frame hidden inside a big coat, a knit cap pulled down tight on her head.

He didn't move on to the next post. Instead he watched as she leaned down to pet her dog and then walked to the barn. He watched as she walked through the doors and a minute later she opened a side door. The horse that ran into the corral took his breath away. Maybe it was the distance, maybe it was the rising sun catching the gold in the red-gold coat, but the animal was crazy beautiful.

Where'd she get a horse like that? How had he missed it last night when he and Brandon had fed the livestock? Right, he'd fed the cattle. Brandon had taken care of the horse, and Gage hadn't thought much about it.

The animal tossed its head and ran around the small enclosure. Layla stood on the outside of the corral, her arms rested on the top rail. The horse changed to a slow, gaited trot that was pretty showy.

Eventually Gage shook his head and went back to work, pounding the next post deeper into the ground. Five more to go. He was down to the second from the last post when Layla walked up to him, her arms crossed and that knit cap making her gray eyes look huge.

"What in the world are you doing?"

He finished the last post, pounding once, twice, three times. He tried to push it, but it was in tight. "Fixing your fence before the cattle realize they can walk right through."

"I can fix my own fences." She looked like a woman about to stomp her foot.

"I know you can. I'm being helpful."

"No, you're feeling guilty. And angry. And I don't know what else. But I am not your problem. You are your problem. Stop trying to fix your life by fixing mine."

He stepped back, stung by her words. She might have a point. "Whatever."

Yeah, that didn't sound much like a teenage girl. He let it go. He had fence to fix. He pulled the tools out of his jacket pocket and grabbed the fence.

"Stop."

He looked up from the wire he was holding and pushed his hat back so he could get a better look at her. He yanked off his sunglasses and shoved them in his pocket. "Why?"

"Because I've got to get ready for church, and if Brandon sees you out here, he isn't going to want to go."

"He'll go."

"Because you'll make him?" She nearly smiled. The edge of her mouth pulled up, and her eyes sparkled just briefly. It took him by surprise, that almost smile.

He shook off the strange urge to hug her and went back to work, ignoring her as she continued to yammer at him, telling him why he was about as low on the food chain as a guy could get.

Finally she did something that sounded a lot like a growl and then she punched him on the arm. He swallowed down a laugh and turned to look at her. She was madder than spit.

"Are you about finished abusing me?"

She yanked off her knit cap and shoved it into her pocket, setting her light brown hair free to drift across her face, set in motion by a light breeze. "No, I'm not done. If you don't get off my property, I'm calling the police."

"You're going to turn me in for fixing your fence?"

"Yes." She bit down on her bottom lip and the angry look in her eyes melted. "You make me so mad."

"Because I'm cute and hard to hate."

"Something like that." Her mouth opened like a landed trout. "I didn't mean the cute part."

"Of course you did."

"No, I didn't. You think you're cute. I don't."

"I could use a cup of coffee. And where did you get that horse?"

"I don't have coffee. And the horse is mine."

"I know he's yours."

"My old stallion died a few years ago. The filly is the last foal I got from him. Her mother was a pretty Arab that I bought at an auction."

"Seriously?"

"Yes, seriously. I had to sell the mare, but I kept the foal. She's three now."

They were walking toward the house at this point. Gage didn't know exactly how it happened. Maybe she started to walk away and he followed. Or maybe they both started walking as they talked about the mare. It didn't really matter; it just meant he was losing it. No big deal.

As they got closer to the house, he glanced toward the corral and the mare that now stood at the opposite side of the enclosure. He whistled and the horse turned, her ears twitching at the sound. She trotted across the enclosure, her legs coming high off the ground in the prettiest dance he'd ever seen. Her neck was arched and her black tail flagged behind her.

"Nice, isn't she?" Layla looked at the horse with obvious pride.

"What are you going to do with her?"

"I had planned to train her for Western pleasure, but then I realized she was a barrel racer." She shrugged slim shoulders beneath the oversize canvas coat. "I don't know…I might sell her."

"Why would you do that?"

She didn't look at him. He guessed if she did, he'd see tears in her eyes. He didn't know what he'd do if faced with those tears.

Layla hadn't meant to tell him that she planned on selling Pretty Girl. But the words had slipped out, her emotions were strung tight and she had confided in the last person on earth she should have been confiding in.

"Layla?"

She shrugged.

"I don't have the money to haul her around the country or the time to train her. She really deserves to be a national champion." She stumbled over all of the reasons she'd been telling herself. When she looked up, he was looking at the mare and not at her. She breathed a sigh of relief. She didn't need to see sympathy in his eyes.

"I'll buy her."

"No." She practically shouted the word and then felt silly.

This time he looked at her. "Really?"

"No, not really. I don't know. Maybe I won't have to get rid of her. Vera said I could work nights waiting tables at The Mad Cow."

The owner of the local diner had always been good to Layla. When the job opened, Layla had jumped on it. Yes, it added one more thing to her to-do list, but it would bring in a little extra money at Christmastime.

"When are you going to start working for Vera?"

She walked up to the corral and reached up to pet Pretty Girl's velvety nose. The mare nuzzled against her palm, her breath warm, her lips twitching and soft. The mare was her dream horse. But dreams changed.

A hand, strong and firm rested on Layla's back. She wanted to shift away from the touch, but she couldn't. Not even when the hand rested on her shoulder, his strong arm encircling her.

"Don't get rid of her, Layla."

Why did his voice have to be so soft, so sincere?

Buck up, Layla. She gave herself the stern lecture and moved from his embrace. "I need to get ready for church."

"I'm going to finish that fence." He reached for her arm and she stopped. "Layla, don't give up."

"I won't." She smiled and backed away from him. "And thank you, for the fence, for talking. I'll see you later."

He waved and then headed back to the fence he'd been working on. She watched him go before she hurried across the yard to the house to finish getting ready. As she headed to her room she yelled at Brandon to get up. He wasn't skipping church. She heard him mutter that he was awake.

She'd give him ten minutes.

Now she had to figure out what she would wear to church. She opened her closet and rummaged through the clothes. A stack of notebooks on the bottom of the closet caught her attention. She hadn't looked at them in years. She didn't plan on looking at them now. Who needed voices from the past to remind them how it felt to have a broken heart?

That girl of sixteen was long gone. She had work-callused hands, a heart that didn't have time for romance and bills to be paid at the first of the month.

At a quarter to ten she walked through the house, carrying the boots she would wear with her denim skirt and searching for her Bible and her brother. She found her Bible on the table next to the chair she'd fallen asleep in two nights ago. She didn't find Brandon.

She slipped her feet into her boots and grabbed a jacket off the hook next to the door. She knew where she'd find her brother. And she was right. He was down at the fence with Gage.

After tossing her purse and Bible in the truck, she walked down to where the two were working away, laughing and talking like old friends. She watched as Brandon pulled the wire tight and Gage clipped it to the metal post.

"It's time to go to church." Layla shivered in the cool morning air.

"I'm going to stay here and help Gage." Brandon didn't even look up. But Gage met her eyes and she glared, letting him know this was his fault.

"You're going to church." Layla cleared her throat and stood a little taller. "Come on."

"Layla, Gage doesn't go to church, so I'm not going."

She heard Gage groan. She shot him another disgusted look.

He sighed.

"Guess I'm going today," Gage grumbled, clipping the last strand of wire. "Come on, kid, before you get us both in trouble."

Brandon looked from Gage, whom he had obviously counted on to be his ally, to Layla. "Seriously, you're giving in to her. Just like that?"

"Just like that."

"I'm not dressed for church." Brandon tried the argument, and Layla knew it was because she always made him put on his best jeans and shirt for church.

Gage wasn't dressed for church, either. His jeans were faded and ripped at the knees. His boots were covered in mud. He obviously hadn't shaved in a couple of days.

"Don't look at me like that," Gage shot back at Layla, probably because of the once-over she'd given him. "We're going to church, and this is how we're going. Besides, I'm about ready to sit down."

"So church is a good place to get warm and put your leg up?"

He laughed, a rich, velvety laugh. "You said it. And I'm driving."

"We're not going to church together." Layla found herself walking next to him, and even feeling a little bit sorry for him because he walked slower than normal. When she glanced up, she saw his mouth tighten in pain.

"You're riding with me. And after church, I'm pretty sure my mom will insist on you all coming over for lunch."

"That should be a good reason for me to take my truck, so that you don't get stuck with us at lunch."

"Layla. Stop arguing for five minutes. Please?"

She stopped, because he looked as if he needed a break. When they reached his truck, he limped around to the passenger side and opened the door for her. Brandon climbed in the back without an argument. She wanted to be mad, but instead she felt a little jealous. After fighting with her brother the past couple of years about everything, he was suddenly compliant, and it had to do with Gage Cooper.

He had a way of bringing people to his side. She remembered back to high school, even in grade school. Gage had always had a crowd of friends. She'd seen him step between friends who were about to go at it, and somehow, with a few words and an easy smile, manage to settle things.

"You know this is going to start rumors, right?" she said as she reached for the seat belt while he got in behind the wheel.

"Oh, well." He turned to the backseat and Brandon. "Is there a pair of boots back there?"

Brandon handed him a pair of boots, beautiful deep brown leather with perfect stitching. Gage took them with a grumbled thank-you. While the truck warmed up, he jerked off his mud-covered boots, grimacing as he pulled the shoe off his left leg. Layla started to tell him he didn't need to fix fences, babysit her brother or drive them to church. He needed to slow down and get better.

But she let it go. If he worked off whatever he was going through, whatever he wanted to change in his life, he'd soon ride off into the sunset and leave her alone. Again. The sooner he was out of her life, the better she'd be.

She grabbed the mud-covered boots he'd taken off and handed them back to Brandon as Gage pulled on the other pair. He now looked like a cowboy who'd been riding range in his best boots. The image made her smile.

A few minutes later they were pulling into the parking lot of the Dawson Community Church. People turned to look at them. Layla resisted the urge to slump down in the seat.

"Are you trying to hide?" Gage pulled into a parking space. Killing the engine, he looked at her.

"I'm not." She sat up straight.

"Yeah, you are. Worried about how it will look, you showing up to church with someone like me?"

She shook her head and reached for the door handle. Brandon was already out and headed across the parking lot. Layla watched him go, focusing on his retreating back and not the man sitting next to her, smelling of the outdoors, soap and ranch.

"Layla, I get that I'm the last person you want to be seen with." He laughed a little. "Sometimes I'm the last person *I* want to be seen with. But you need a little help with your brother and with the farm. I know people have tried to help you over the years and you've said you could do it all yourself. Well, I'm not as willing to believe that as everyone else. Or maybe I'm just not as willing to be run off."

"I've noticed." She smiled and opened her door. "They're ringing the bell."

He wasn't willing to be run off. Yeah, she got it. But she was counting on the fact that eventually he'd get bored. Or the lure of the road would pull him away.

As she walked across the parking lot to the pretty country church that she'd attended most of her life, she thought that maybe he wasn't the worst thing that had happened to her. Brandon was in church this morning. He'd stayed home last night. And he'd talked about his plans for the week, about going to Cooper Creek Ranch after school and what he'd learned from Jackson Cooper about cattle.

It could be worse.

As she walked, Gage limped fast to catch up with her. He reached her side, shooting her a look that she didn't dwell on. They were going up the steps and Slade McKennon was at the door, the way he always was, handing out church bulletins. He handed her a bulletin, and then gave one to Gage. He looked from one to the other of them, his eyes narrowing.

"I was helping her fix some fences," Gage explained as they walked through the door.

"I don't need an explanation," Slade whispered as they walked into the church.

Gage took hold of her arm and pulled her to the Cooper family pew, sliding her in right next to Granny Myrna Cooper, the biggest matchmaker in the county.

Everyone knew that Myrna Cooper had taken it upon herself to give each of her grandchildren one of her heirloom rings. Mia Cooper and her fiancé, Slade McKennon, had been the latest recipients of one of Myrna's rings. Before that, Jesse Cooper and his new wife, Laura.

A person with a lick of sense wouldn't want to give Myrna any ideas about where her next ring might find a home.

But obviously Gage didn't have much sense.

Chapter Five

He should have seen it coming. Nearly his entire family was standing on the sidewalk after church. Of course they invited Layla and Brandon to lunch, as he'd known they would. He'd counted on it, actually. But the curious looks from his family, and from people leaving the church, those he hadn't counted on.

Couldn't a guy just be nice and help someone out?

And then he heard his mom invite Layla and Brandon to join them on the wagon ride in the fields. Today?

"That isn't until next week." Gage jumped into the conversation, trying to stop this runaway train before it sped away from him.

His mom shot him a warning look. "The weather is supposed to get bad so we decided to go today."

His grandmother sidled up next to him, her smile making him more than a little nervous. That grin on Granny Myrna's face meant one thing. She'd taken to matchmaking again. Couldn't her own engagement be enough for her? And where was Winston, anyway?

"You're making this a lot easier than I thought you would," his grandmother whispered loudly. Like she thought no one would hear, but everyone did, and those standing closest to him laughed.

He opened his mouth to object, but he couldn't think how to stop his grandmother. And if he said too much, he'd hurt Layla. He didn't want to hurt her, but people needed to realize that Layla was the kind of woman a man married.

He normally stayed as far away from the marrying kind of women as he could. A waitress at a café in Texas, a secretary in Arizona—women who weren't interested in settling down.

He wasn't a terrible person; he just didn't want to lead anyone on. He'd done that in high school, to Layla. He'd been filled with regret ever since.

And as soon as his leg healed up, he planned on heading out of Dawson. He'd been thinking he might like to hang out in New Mexico for a while. A friend had some bucking bulls down there and he'd asked Gage to help him out, maybe stay at his ranch for a while.

"Your eyes are glazing over," Granny Myrna whispered close to his ear. "They're discussing having you drive one of the wagons."

"Good." He shifted the weight off his leg. When he glanced around he realized they'd lost Brandon. "Where'd the kid go?"

Layla answered him from where she stood, next to his sister Mia. "He went home with Lewis Marler's family."

"Lewis? Is that a good idea?" He looked from Layla to various members of his family, because no one seemed concerned by the news that Brandon had taken off with some kid named Lewis Marler.

"He's fine." Layla stiffened slim shoulders and turned away from him.

Next to him, his grandmother laughed a little and she might have whispered a warning, telling him to tread slowly. He ignored the laughter and the warning.

"You think?" he said. Layla shot him a warning look, the kind that if she'd been a cat would have been accompanied by a warning twitch of her tail.

"Yes, Gage, I think."

"So, I guess we should all head on out to the ranch." Jackson pushed his cowboy hat on his head, slipped an arm around his wife, Madeline, laughed and walked away.

Gage watched as the rest of his family dispersed, including his granny Myrna. They left him standing there with Layla Silver.

He pulled the keys out of his pocket and Layla didn't move. She had pulled a white knit cap down over her hair but strands still blew around cheeks that were now pink from the breeze. Her gray eyes sparkled with moisture and her lips were glossy from the balm she'd just pocketed in her red coat.

She was about the prettiest thing he'd ever seen.

"We should go." He inclined his head in the direction of his truck.

She nodded, and he took that as agreement that they'd be riding together. He guessed he'd hoped she would insist on either going home or riding with someone else. Instead she walked next to him back to his truck, both of them silent.

When they got to the truck he opened the passenger side door for her. She glanced down the road. He figured she was still thinking about Brandon. She brushed hair back from her face, giving Gage a close look at the worry in her eyes.

"He'll be fine," he offered, hoping to take away what looked like the weight of the world on her shoulders.

"That isn't what you thought a few minutes ago. Maybe I shouldn't have let him go."

"No, it isn't. I guess you can't hold a kid hostage."

She nodded and climbed into the truck. Gage stood in the door for a minute, wishing he knew what to say. He wasn't the Cooper who knew the right words to say. He'd never been the Cooper out rescuing damsels in distress, rushing to the aid of neighbors. His brothers had always been better at the white knight thing. He closed the truck door and a moment later got in behind the wheel.

"We can go find him, if you want," he said as he backed out of the parking spot.

"Maybe I should go home?" She bit down on her bottom lip, her gray eyes focused on the road ahead of them.

"Why would you do that? Do you have something you need to do?"

"I always have something that needs to be taken care of. I do need to put plastic over my windows. I need to work with my mare. I should be there to wait for Brandon."

"You can keep coming up with excuses, but I also think you need a break. When I take you home, if Brandon isn't there, we'll go look for him."

A Christmas song played on the radio. Layla listened and she didn't answer Gage for a long time. Finally she shrugged. "I don't feel right, showing up at your house for a family event. It's your family. It's a Christmas tradition that you all do together."

"I think my mom is more excited about you joining us than she is about me being there," he offered, smiling at her before turning his attention back to the road.

"Thank you, that's nice of you to say."

"I'm not just saying it. Another Cooper family tradition is that we love to include people. It wouldn't be Christmas if we didn't have a big crowd."

He turned onto the drive that led up to the Cooper house. Layla looked about ready to jump out of her skin. Yeah, he got it; this place probably did look a little overwhelming to someone who wasn't used to it. He remembered the look on Mia's face when she first joined their family. He'd only been a little kid but he had watched from the crowd as they gathered to greet their new sister.

Layla wasn't like Mia. His sister had never been quiet, not really. Once she'd gotten used to their family, she'd pushed her way through life. Layla did what she had to do with a quietness that he wasn't used to.

But, like Mia, she didn't seem to want people in her business. She wanted to do it all on her own.

"It has to get exhausting," he murmured, not really planning to say it out loud.

"What?"

He pulled in next to Jackson's truck. "Being you. It has to be exhausting. You've been a grown-up your whole life, haven't you?"

Her lips parted and she blinked. Oh, great, she was going to cry. He hadn't meant to make her cry. He ran a hand through his hair, trying to come up with something to lighten the mood.

"You've been carrying the load alone, not really letting people help." He groaned, because that wasn't any better.

"People help." She reached for the door handle, fumbling to find it. He leaned across, moved her hand and opened the door. She leaned back into her seat to avoid his arm.

He couldn't avoid her scent. Couldn't avoid meeting those serious eyes of hers. It took him back to that day in the cafeteria when he'd asked her to be his tutor in chemistry. She'd given him that serious look. He'd flirted, smiled, maybe winked, and finally she'd agreed.

Then he remembered the look in her eyes the day she'd walked around the corner of the hallway and saw him with her best friend. He'd just kissed Cheryl and looked up to see Layla, eyes wide with pain.

In that moment he'd realized what he'd done to her. It had been eating at him for years. Back then he'd tried to tell her she was too good for him. It had only been words at the time, but as time went on, he'd realized how right he'd been.

She was still too good for him. But that didn't stop him from wanting to kiss her. Once upon a time she'd tutored him in chemistry. He was thinking seriously about returning the favor.

Layla saw the look in his eyes change. He'd leaned over to help her with the door because she'd suddenly lost the ability to find a door handle. But something happened. The air got sucked out of the truck, everything stopped, and as he moved to sit back up, his gaze locked with hers.

Layla pushed the door open and fled the confines of

the truck, nearly bumping into Travis Cooper and his wife, Elizabeth. Travis grabbed her arms to steady her.

"Whoa there." He grinned and let her go. "Trying to run will only make him chase faster. He's a lot like a dog after a rabbit that way. Better to freeze and hope he doesn't see you."

Elizabeth's mouth dropped and she gasped. "Travis, enough."

Layla couldn't agree more. She looked around, rethinking the desire to run, considering the advice Travis had given her, and then wishing she'd brought her own truck. Elizabeth put an arm around her waist. Layla moved from the touch but she smiled at the other woman, hoping she'd understand.

"They're like Labrador pups—they can be overwhelming, but they mean well." Elizabeth should know, she'd once been an only child growing up in St. Louis. Now she had a baby, a husband who could charm stars from the sky and an extended family that filled two pews at the Dawson Community Church.

"I know they mean well." Layla watched as Gage walked away with Travis, leaving her to walk with Elizabeth and the baby in her arms.

"Gage will push back if they push too hard," Elizabeth offered.

"That's good to know." Layla started to say Gage helping her would be a temporary hobby. He'd soon move on.

He'd get in his truck and take off, the way he sometimes did. She'd been at the Convenience Counts convenience store when he filled his truck with gas this summer, bought a few candy bars and a bottle of water before heading out.

Trish, the owner, had asked where he was going. He'd given her that easy smile and told her wherever the wind took him.

She'd been jealous, wondering what that would be like, to take off and leave problems and responsibilities behind. She'd tried, years ago. She'd gone to college, thinking she'd graduate and never come back to Dawson. But her parents' deaths had changed all of that. She'd come home, and she would never leave.

"Are you okay?" Elizabeth asked as they got closer to the house.

"I'm fine."

They walked up the steps. Gage had waited on the porch for them, pushed the front door open and held it, his gaze remaining on Layla. When they entered the house Elizabeth left her alone with Gage. Somewhere Christmas music played, and a voice joined in, a deep bass voice. Tim Cooper, maybe. She smiled, especially when others joined him.

"I'm sorry," Gage whispered close to her ear and she nodded. The smile disappeared.

"It's okay." She shrugged out of her coat and he took it, hanging it with the others on the hall tree at the door.

From the kitchen she heard the laughter and conversation of his big family. She could smell the roast that Angie Cooper had put in the Crock-Pot. Layla imagined there was more than one. With a family this size, would one roast feed them all?

"If you're sure." And then he kissed her cheek.

Her cheek?

He pulled back, and for some reason he looked at her with a kindness that took her by surprise. His hand touched the cheek that he'd kissed and he smiled.

For a moment she wanted to be someone else, someone more exciting, maybe the type of person he could fall in love with. That woman would be free to take off at a moment's notice. She wouldn't have responsibilities or a job at the local feed store.

But Layla wasn't that person. She couldn't leave Dawson at a moment's notice, and she couldn't let herself fall in love with Gage Cooper.

"We should definitely join everyone before they send Granny Myrna to find us."

They both laughed, and Layla felt the tension ease away as she thought about Myrna, legendary matchmaker, and kindest soul in town. As they walked down the hall to join his family, she tried to hold on to that moment.

Lunch with the Coopers kept a person too busy to think. There had been laughter, conversation and too much food. Gage had sat next to her, not really participating in the conversation, but from time to time leaning to say something to Layla, a side note on whatever the family had been discussing.

Gage finally drove her back home that evening after sundown. She had containers of leftovers that Angie had sent along, so she wouldn't have to cook that night. She thought more likely that she wouldn't have to cook for days. She had memories of a perfect afternoon with a family that enjoyed being together, laughing and talking.

She also had memories of sitting next to Gage as he handled the pair of golden-coated draft horses that pulled the wagon. The rest of the family had piled in the back. She had been pushed onto the bench seat next to Gage, a blanket over her legs and a thermos of hot chocolate in her hands and two cups.

The ride had lasted two hours, with the family singing carols, until the sky started to turn gray and the temperature dropped. Layla had shivered in the seat next to Gage, and he'd slipped an arm behind her, pulling her close to his side.

Wonderful memories to cherish.

Now, several hours later, his truck pulled to a stop in front of her house. She saw lights on in the kitchen. She didn't think she'd left them on. Her gaze shot to the barn. She would still have to feed.

"I'll help you."

"What?" She looked at Gage in the dark cab of the truck, his face touched by the glow of the security light near the barn.

"It's cold and it's late. I'll help you take care of your animals."

"Brandon can do it."

"Let's check on Brandon and see how his day went."

He said it in a way that worried her. Why would he be concerned about Brandon's day?

They walked up to the front door. She heard the television and saw the flicker of light from the screen. Gage reached past her to push the door open. They stepped inside, and Layla stopped when she saw her brother stretched out on the floor.

"Brandon!" she called out in concern.

"He's passed out, not dead."

She kneeled next to her brother, feeling the pulse in his neck. He opened his eyes and grinned.

"You stink." She moved away from him.

"I got sick on the porch."

"Just when I think you're going to change."

Brandon frowned and closed his eyes. "I'm not going to change. Remember, I'm just like dad."

She'd said that to him. She sat back, still on the floor. Strong hands rested on her shoulders. She'd told her brother he had to change or he'd be like their father. The words had been harsh, fueled by her anger.

"I'm sorry." She whispered the apology.

But was it too late? She'd spoken this into existence. She'd planted the seed in her brother, hadn't she? She'd been so tired when she'd said it. She'd been worn down and she hadn't known what to do next. She had watched him stagger into the kitchen, just fifteen and drunk, and it had reminded her of their father coming home on a Friday night, his paycheck gone after a trip to the casino, where he'd known that he'd strike it rich.

He'd had many addictions, their father. Once he'd been a bull rider, then a drinker, and then he'd been a gambler.

Those were their family traditions. But she wanted something better and lasting for her and Brandon. Faith—that was the one thing she'd worked at giving her brother. A faith based on the greatest Christmas tradition of all.

"Gage." Coming out of her trance, she turned to him. "You should go."

She wanted to close the door, pull the blinds and pretend they weren't falling apart, the same way she'd pretended years ago. She'd gone to school, worked hard, smiled and pretended.

"I'm going to feed." Gage nudged Brandon with his boot. "Get up. You can help."

"I can't." Brandon covered his face with his arm.

"You will." Gage leaned and grabbed her brother's arm, pulling him to his feet. "You're going to get some fresh air, sober up and grow up."

"I'm only fifteen. I'm not supposed to be grown-up." He staggered a little as he got to his feet.

"Yeah, well, your sister has enough on her plate without you making it worse."

"Whatever, man." Brandon backed up a few steps, then propelled himself to the front door. Layla wanted to cry. She wanted to scream at him.

She stood and went after him, catching him at the front porch.

"Brandon, you don't have to be like him. Like Dad. You don't have to do this."

He glanced back on his way down the steps, his eyes blurry, his smile wavering. He was somewhere between being a boy and a man. What kind of man would he become?

"No, you were right. I'm just like him."

"But I don't want that for you." Layla looked past her brother to the other man standing on her front porch, his hazel eyes full of sympathy. She refocused on Brandon. "You should want more for yourself."

"I don't know, Layla. I'm just messed up." He tumbled down off the porch and would have fallen if Gage hadn't caught him.

She watched them head for the barn, her brother and the man who thought he owed her something. What did she do now?

Chapter Six

She was sitting at the dining room table with a cup of hot tea when Gage walked through her back door thirty minutes later. Brandon had stomped through five minutes earlier. She had tried to talk to him. He'd waved her off and kept walking.

Gage stood in the doorway, his hat pushed back, his mouth a grim line of disgust, or anger. She didn't know which. She pointed to the cup of tea she'd made for him. It was the least she could do.

At this point she didn't think she was going to push him out of her life the way she'd planned a few days earlier. He seemed determined to make things right. Whatever that meant.

He didn't sit down, just stood there looking around the kitchen at everything but her. After a long minute he sighed and reached for the other chair. He pulled it close to hers and sat. Taking off his hat, he tossed it onto the table and ran a hand through his unruly brown hair.

"Why haven't you asked for help?" He leaned back in the chair, watching her with those hazel eyes fringed with dark lashes, maybe seeing more than most people.

She looked up, blinking fast to clear moisture that skimmed her eyes, blurring her vision. What did she say to that question? Did she tell him about the bruises her mom had hidden, or about cleaning her dad up after a drunken night and not telling anyone? Maybe she should tell him about cleaning hotel rooms at fifteen to keep the lights on. But her family had never talked about those things, not even with each other.

When she took over as head of the family, she'd kept the tradition of keeping things to herself. People had often asked if she needed anything, if things were going okay, and she always smiled and said everything was fine.

And they'd allowed her that illusion, even though from time to time a bill was paid anonymously or meat was provided by a neighbor who said they had too much.

Now, with Gage looking at her so intently, she shut down.

"Plenty of people have helped us."

"Yeah, when you let them." His hand slipped through his hair again and he shook his head. "Brandon needs help, Layla."

"I know." She brushed at her eyes, felt moisture that she wouldn't let fall. "I know."

"Why don't you talk to Wyatt Johnson?"

The pastor of Dawson Community Church. She'd thought about it. First she had to admit that they had a problem. Her dad had tried a twelve-step program once, thinking he might get clean. The problem was she didn't want people knowing that she wasn't okay, that she wasn't handling this. She was hiding the same way an addict hid.

"I'll think about it." She glanced at the clock on the wall in front of her. "It's late. You should go."

He nodded and pushed himself up, using the rickety old table as leverage. It creaked beneath his weight. She stood, because she should follow him to the door. She needed to thank him for helping, even if it was about him more than it was about them.

They walked through the tiny living room, warm from the fire in the fireplace. She could hear Brandon in his room. At the door, Gage took her coat off the hook and handed it to her. She didn't ask; she just slipped it on. Without questioning him or herself, she followed Gage outside.

Cold air brushed her heated cheeks. Layla walked down off the porch and looked up at the clear sky. Christmas was coming.

Gage's hand closed over hers. He led her across the yard to his truck. She should pull her hand from his and go back to the house. Alone. But she was so tired of being alone, of shouldering everything on her own.

She was letting Gage make amends, because he needed it. She was letting him make amends because it had been so long since someone took part of the load from her shoulders.

At the back of her mind she remembered who he was. Gage hadn't ever been the responsible Cooper. But his hand was tight on hers, strong, warm. How did a girl pull away from a touch that made her feel safe?

Safe and Gage. The two didn't go together.

They neared his truck, snow flurries falling cold against the warm skin of her face. She felt hot and chilled all at once. She couldn't get sick, not now, not when she needed her job.

"If you want, I can talk to Wyatt." Gage's voice broke through the wild chain of thoughts rushing through her mind.

"What?" Oh, Brandon. "Yes. Let me think about it."

"Now is the time to get him help."

"Gage, thank you, but I'll take care of it."

"Right, of course. Because you like to keep the doors barred and people out of your life." His eyes narrowed. "I saw once, you know."

"Saw what?"

"A bruise on your cheek. You tried to hide it with makeup. And when our math teacher asked you about it, you said you tripped and hit your cheek on the table."

Shame heated her cheeks. She looked away from him, but his fingers touched her chin, turning her to face him.

"I need to go inside." She shivered in the cool, damp air.

"Not before I do this." He leaned in, and she didn't dare to breathe, even knowing she couldn't let him kiss her. She shook her head. He pulled her close and held her. She was tight against his chest, his strong arms around her, his hands on her back.

"Gage," she whispered into the warm flannel of his shirt. His heartbeat beneath her ear was steady. He was warm and solid.

She shouldn't have stayed in his arms, held against him, but she couldn't stop the need from rising up inside her, the need to be held. For those few moments she felt safe. Like someone was in this with her. Her heart didn't care if it was Gage.

"I'm going to help you, Layla. We're going to get things settled around here. I won't go anywhere until we

have things fixed up, and Brandon on the right track."
He whispered the words close to her ear, then brushed
a kiss across her cheek.

He wouldn't go anywhere, until... She needed to pull
back. His words were a reminder that he couldn't be the
person she counted on. Just one more moment in his
arms. He kissed the top of her head and then she drew
back, leaving the warmth of his embrace.

"I should go."

He peered down at her. "Are you sick?"

"No, why?"

"You look pale."

"It's winter and I have fair skin. Of course I look
pale."

He brushed a hand across her cheek. "You feel
warm."

"I'm fine."

The snow fell harder and she pulled her light jacket
tight to keep out the chill. It wouldn't snow long, just
enough to be pretty. Gage had pushed his hat down
low over his eyes.

"I really should go." He reached for the door of his
truck. "If you need anything at all, call me."

She nodded, but she wouldn't call him. She didn't
call people. He grinned and shook his head because
he knew.

"Goodbye." She backed away from him.

"I mean it, about calling. I know you won't, but I
mean it."

She nodded and then headed back to the house. The
dog met her on the front porch, wanting inside.

She reached for the doorknob as Daisy jumped
around her, barking at the closed door. Gage's head-

lights flashed across the porch as he backed out to turn around. The dog barked again, and Layla walked in the front door.

Brandon was asleep. She glanced at the clock and shook her head. It was too early, but she let it go. He had school in the morning. She had work.

She flipped on the hall light and headed for her room, the one bedroom upstairs. It was freezing cold. Sometimes it was so cold that a glass of water would freeze on her bedside table before morning. But she loved the room in the eaves. It had been a part of the original home, back when her ancestors had first settled in Indian Territory, taking advantage of government land, the railroad and the river.

It had been her sanctuary. It still was.

She changed quickly and then reached into the closet for her robe. Once again she spotted the notebooks that held her journals. She should read a book, not a journal from years ago. But she grabbed the one on top. Just a quick peek.

Big mistake. She shook her head as she read entries that detailed her crush on Gage Cooper. Yikes, she had doodled his name and hers. She had recorded prayers. Some for her family, friends and people in Dawson. And one for Gage, that he would love her.

The journal of Layla Silver, sappy teenager, delusional, hopeless romantic. Back when she'd once believed in fairy tales and happy-ever-afters.

She tossed the journal back into the dark depths of her closet and grabbed a romance novel off her bookcase. Much better to lose herself in fiction than get lost in the past.

When she walked downstairs, Brandon was in the

kitchen rummaging through the fridge and pulling out Angie Cooper's leftovers.

He looked at her, his eyes somber and sheepish. He shrugged. "I'm a jerk."

"Yes, you can be." Why should she disagree? She took the leftovers and started dishing them up on two plates. "But I love you and I worry about you."

"I know." He looked down at the floor. He was a kid. A six-foot-tall kid in worn jeans and a hoodie. He still had acne and his hair always needed to be washed.

He probably needed hugs, too. When was the last time she'd hugged him? It had been years. She remembered him as a little boy needing their mom. She'd still needed her, too. But she'd done her best. She'd hugged him a lot back then. Mrs. Phelps, his babysitter when Layla worked, had hugged him, too.

She put her arms around him and held him tight for a long minute. He protested and squirmed.

"What are you doing?" He tried to move out of her arms.

"I think you need a hug."

He groaned but then he gave her a quick hug back before escaping. "There, are you happy? I hugged you. Just don't tell anyone."

She smiled and they both laughed a little. "I won't."

"Good, because that was weird."

"Brandon, I want you to talk to Pastor Johnson. Wyatt is a good man. He's been through a lot. Maybe we should both talk to him." She pulled a plate out of the microwave and stood there, looking at her little brother who now towered over her.

He shrugged and took the heated plate from her

hands. On his way to the table he mumbled that he'd think about it.

They'd been falling apart for a long time. She wondered how Gage Cooper, a man who barely seemed in control of his own life, was the one forcing them to fix their broken lives.

She reminded herself that he'd used her before to get what he wanted. He no longer wanted to date her best friend, or help with chemistry, though.

He wanted to be a better person. She couldn't fault him for that. But she also couldn't let herself fall in love with him. Not this time.

Thoughts of Gage fled, because she noticed the pile of mail she'd dropped on the counter the day before, and then forgot about. She sifted through the envelopes, wishing that she hadn't. The day had been long enough without adding to the stress. She took one envelope from the pile and walked out of the room with it.

If Brandon wondered why, he didn't ask.

Gage walked through the barn at Cooper Creek on Monday morning. Limped, actually. His knee was swollen and sore. Too much time on his feet. The doctor had warned him to take it easy. He'd always had a hard time sitting still. Listening wasn't actually one of his best traits, either.

The door opened. He turned, smiling when he saw Reese walk through the door, his white cane swinging in front of him as he traversed the dark world he'd lived in since returning from Afghanistan.

"Anyone here?" Reese kept walking, smiling as he moved forward.

Reese never seemed to get angry. Or bitter. But Gage

had been bitter enough for both of them. Why would God let this happen to Reese? Reese, who always helped others, unlike Gage, who skipped out.

Gage had a lot of anger, because if God was going to punish someone, it might as well be him and not his brother. He could admit to himself that he'd been taking a lot of chances for that very reason.

"Hello?" Reese called out again.

"I'm here." Gage turned away from his brother, the way he'd been doing for the past year. "I'm going to work that new gelding."

"Is he any good?"

"Good as most," Gage answered, walking down the aisle between the stalls and stopping in front of a dark chestnut gelding. The deep red of the horse's coat caught the sunlight from the open window. The animal moved to the stall door, shoving his head at Gage. He ran a hand down the sleek neck.

The horse made him think of the mare he'd seen at Layla's. She had a prize horse and he doubted many people knew it.

"You still here?" Reese walked up, his cane tapping the stall door.

"I'm still here."

"Good to have you back."

"Yeah." He snapped a lead rope to the horse's halter.

"Gage, it's time for us to talk. You've been mad long enough. I'm not sure if it's something I've done or if someone else made you mad. But I do know you can't keep running off every time someone says something that gets under your skin."

"I'm not running."

"Not this time?" Reese reached and the horse nuzzled his hand.

"Not for the time being. I'm going to put a few things right."

"Meaning?"

"There are people I've hurt, people I've done things to. It's time to make amends."

"Right, I'm not going to argue with you about that. But that doesn't tell me why you've avoided me like the plague." Reese stopped, a slow smile spreading across his face. "You afraid you'll catch blindness?"

"No." Two years ago, they probably would have been in a fight by now. He would have pushed Reese. Reese would have pushed back. They would have been rolling in the aisle of the stable until someone stopped them.

"You itching to hit me?" Reese asked.

"Probably so." Gage smiled a little as he said it.

"Then do it. Hit me."

"Right."

"Because you can't hit a blind guy?" Reese grinned and reached, pushing Gage just a little.

"Don't."

"Don't start it if you can't finish it, Gage. If you're going to be mad, I'll give you something to be mad about."

Gage pushed back and Reese took a step, then found his balance. He laughed, but Gage wasn't amused. Reese was baiting him—he knew, and he should let it go.

"It should have been me." He leaned in close and the words came out gruff. Reese shook his head, clearly not getting it.

"What should have been you?" Reese stepped close, his smile gone.

"If someone should have gotten hurt, it should have been me. Not you."

Reese took off his sunglasses and shoved them in the pocket of his shirt. He stood there for a long minute, staring in Gage's direction, and then he shook his head.

"You've got to be kidding. All of this anger is over my blindness? What, you think God looked down one day and thought He ought to smite someone, so He picked me? But He messed up, because you would have been a better target?" Reese used his cane to find the bench next to the office. He sat down. "I don't know if I should laugh or knock you down."

"I don't think you can take me."

"I think I can. This isn't a punishment, Gage. It's life. It's a new path and a new challenge. It's opened doors for me to share my story, and my faith."

"Yeah, I get that." Gage sat down next to his brother, rubbing his knee. "I'm not an idiot."

"No, you just play one in the movies."

"Shut up. I know that God isn't looking for people to punish."

"You were angry because you thought I deserved better." Reese grinned and then laughed. "Because you think I'm that righteous. That's pretty good."

"Shut up."

"I will, if you'll tell me what's going on with Layla Silver."

"I'm helping her out. She needs the help."

"I think she's always done a decent job of holding things together."

"That's what everyone thinks." Gage leaned back,

resting his head on the rough wall of the stable. Was he the only one who could see that she was barely holding on? "I didn't plan on helping her…it just happened."

"Gotcha. Well, if you're planning on skipping out of here anytime soon, just remember that she's a…"

"Nester."

"Yeah."

Gage knew that. He had no intentions of getting tied up with someone looking for a ring and a walk down the aisle. He had plans. In a few months he was heading to New Mexico. He'd stay and help his friend with his new bucking bulls. That might take six months. He might even buy a few bulls of his own to add to Jerry's herd.

He also planned on returning to bull riding as soon as the doctor gave him the okay. He was still young. He'd won the finals. Next time he'd win the world title.

"Gage, seriously, you have to get past the anger."

"I'm working on it."

"Right, okay." Reese stood and unfolded his cane. "I came out to find you and tell you I'm going to be a dad again."

"No way." Gage stood and clasped his brother's hand.

"Yeah, way. Listen, Gage, I'm not angry with God. Don't you be angry for me."

Gage knew he had to get past this. It wasn't that easy.

"I'm happy for you and Cheyenne."

"Thanks." Reese cocked his head to the side. "Still angry?"

"I'm working on that, so give me a break."

"Fine. Mom wanted you to know she's going to Tulsa with Dad. You're on your own for lunch and dinner."

"I think I can handle feeding myself."

"Don't tell her that. She'll think you don't need her."

Gage laughed and walked back to the gelding. "She knows we all need her. Lucky is knocking on the door of forty, and he still comes over for lunch." Their older brother, Lucky had been married since his junior year in college.

"Yeah, she wouldn't know what to do if he didn't." Reese headed for the door. "I have to find Cheyenne and get back to town. Could you try to stay out of trouble?"

"I'm trying."

Gage watched his brother go. It was hard, letting him walk away without offering to help. But Reese knew where he was going, what he was doing, and he knew how to make it through the world, even blind.

Gage had been in church the first time Reese spoke, telling everyone that blindness meant trusting. He had to trust the people in his life. He had to trust that there was nothing in his path when he walked through the house. He had to trust that obstacles would be moved. He had to trust the cane and his other senses. More than anything, he had to trust God.

He'd said that everyone should trust God as if they were blind.

Gage had been angry when he'd listened. He hadn't gotten it. He hadn't gotten how God could do this to his brother. How Reese could be so accepting. Now, watching his brother navigate a dark world, trusting his senses, trusting the cane, maybe now he did. Or at least he was starting to.

He guessed if he'd been Reese, he would have been fighting mad. He would have fought the darkness. He would have fought the cane. He would have hit a lot of walls and bumped into a lot of obstacles.

The irony of that hit him head-on. He *had* been hitting obstacles and bumping into walls.

Chapter Seven

Layla left the feed store at five o'clock Monday afternoon and walked across the street to the Mad Cow Café. Vera had offered her a job a couple of nights a week. One of her waitresses was pregnant and on bed rest. The job wouldn't be permanent, but it would get her through the holidays.

Her feet ached as she made the block and a half trek to the restaurant in the concrete block building, painted with black-and-white spots like a Holstein cow. As she walked she inhaled the aroma of Vera's fried chicken. She watched as a few of the town council members strung lights and hung lighted candy canes from electric poles. Christmas was coming. It made her hopeful. But it also worried her because she never knew how she'd make the holiday a good one for her brother. Not that he'd ever really seemed to care. But she cared enough for both of them.

The parking lot was crowded. Older farmers were there early to make sure they got Vera's famous fried chicken before it was sold out.

When she walked through the doors of the only diner

in Dawson, several people turned to wave and call out a greeting. She returned the greeting and went in search of Vera. She found her in the kitchen, turning chicken that she fried in cast-iron skillets.

"Hey, girl, good of you to come over and help." Vera wiped her hands on a rag and straightened her hairnet. "We're swamped already."

Vera handed her tongs over to the other cook, and motioned for Layla to follow her.

"You're assuming I know how to wait tables." Layla followed Vera out the swinging doors and back into the dining area.

"Oh, honey, you've been here enough, you know the drill. The only thing you won't know is the abbreviations, so don't try. I'll have Breezy show you the ropes on the first couple of tables and then you'll be on your own."

Breezy Hernandez turned from the table she'd been waiting on. She was Mia Cooper's long-lost biological sister.

"Hey, Layla. I'm glad to see you." Breezy hurried past with an order to turn in.

Vera grinned. "That girl has more energy than ten of me. She's doing a great job with the music on Saturdays, too."

"So I've heard."

Vera handed Layla an apron, order pad and a pen. "Good luck."

She would need more than luck. Monday night at the Mad Cow was crazy. The tables filled, emptied and refilled. Layla took orders, stopped to talk when she could, made salads and then did it all over again.

"Layla, when did you start working here?" Slade

McKennon, in his police uniform, opened a menu. It was thirty minutes until closing time and the café had cleared out, leaving just a few tables to wait on.

"Vera needed a little help." She pulled out her order pad.

"That's great." He looked over the menu and then set it down. "She's out of chicken, right?"

"Sorry."

"No problem, I'll have a chef salad with ranch dressing. Coffee to drink."

Layla wrote down the order and started to walk away. Slade touched her arm. She saw he wasn't smiling.

She let out a long sigh. "Brandon?"

"Afraid so. Don't worry, this isn't official, but I wanted you to know that we had a report of some kids driving recklessly on Back Street yesterday afternoon."

She didn't need more information. "It was probably him."

"I'd like to help, if I can. I know Gage has him out at the ranch this afternoon."

That was news to her. She must have made a face because Slade grinned.

"Gage is trying to be helpful." She didn't mean to say it like she didn't appreciate his help. She did. She just didn't need this much Gage Cooper in her life.

Why in the world did she always love the bad boys? Her mom had said it was in her genes, that she had to fight it and find a good boy who would stay close to home, love Jesus and work hard.

She hardly thought Gage qualified.

Slade cleared his throat, an obvious attempt to stop her woolgathering, she guessed. She took his menu.

"Gage gets him, Layla. And maybe helping Brandon will help Gage find himself."

She didn't comment on that. "I'll get this order in.

Slade nodded and before he could say anything else, his phone rang. As she walked through the doors to the kitchen, Slade yelled out to cancel his order. He had to leave. Layla tossed the paper in the trash. When she returned to the dining room, Slade was gone, blue lights flashing as he took off.

"It's closing time, girls." Vera walked out of the kitchen, drying her hands on a towel.

Layla's feet couldn't have agreed more. She seriously needed a massage. And better shoes. She hobbled over to the door and turned off the neon Open sign.

"You okay?" Breezy slipped the apron off her waist and tossed it under the counter at the front of the dining room. She reached for Layla's.

"I'm good. Just worn-out."

"It won't take long to clean up our work area," Breezy offered with another big smile. "I already filled the condiments for the morning shift."

"I don't know how you do it."

"I don't work two jobs," Breezy said matter-of-factly.

"You girls head on home. Frank's here, and we'll get things cleaned up." Vera pushed a button on the register. "Layla, you did good tonight."

"Thanks, Vera."

Breezy pushed the door open. The two of them stepped outside. It was colder than cold. Layla shivered and pushed her hands deep into her pocket.

"Where's your truck?" Breezy looked around, eyeing the parking lot, empty except for Vera's Jeep.

"I left it at the feed store. I guess I should have driven

it over here, but when I left work it seemed easier to leave it."

"I'd give you a ride, but I'm walking." Breezy lived with Mia, until Mia and Slade got married. "I guess we can walk together."

They walked in easy silence most of the way. The town was quiet, just one lonely truck driving past. The Christmas lights swayed in the breeze. Breezy seemed to have a lot on her mind. Layla enjoyed the peace and quiet. It had been a long day. When they got to the parking lot of the feed store, they stopped.

"I'll wait while you get in your truck." Breezy offered, glancing around the dark area.

"I'm fine. It's Dawson. Besides, you still have another block to go." She pulled her keys out of her purse. "I could give you a ride so you don't have to walk in the dark."

Breezy laughed an easy laugh. "If you had seen some of the places I've slept, you'd know I'm not worried."

Layla said a silent thank-you. At least she'd always had a home. Breezy hadn't been so lucky.

"Breezy, thank you for helping me out tonight. I didn't expect it to wear me out."

"You'd already worked a long day. It had to be exhausting."

"It was. I'm sure it'll get easier."

They parted. Breezy walked down the sidewalk, looked back once and waved. Layla climbed into her truck, happy to sit down, even in the cold cab. She stuck the key in the ignition and cranked.

Nothing happened. She groaned and tried again. This couldn't be happening. Not tonight. Not in this cold. She'd walked home before when her truck hadn't

started, but it had been warm and during the day. She
didn't want to walk tonight. And Breezy didn't have a
car to give her a ride.

She sat for a minute, waiting. She tried again and
nothing happened, not even a click. The gas tank wasn't
empty. She knew it wasn't. Her battery was nearly new.
She tried once more, with the same horrible results.

She'd have to walk. But she really didn't want to.
She stood in the gravel parking lot, looking around the
dimly lit area and wishing like crazy she hadn't turned
off service to her cell phone. But she couldn't afford it.
There were a lot of things she couldn't afford.

She couldn't afford to fix this old truck. She couldn't
afford to get sick. She couldn't afford the payments on
the loan she'd taken out on the farm. But she'd had to
do it. They'd needed a new roof. The farm had been
paid off and the bank had felt secure giving her a line
of credit. She'd had her job in Grove for six years.

Who would have thought she'd lose it a month after
getting the loan?

With no other options, she headed down the road
in the direction of the farm. She glanced at her watch,
shivering with cold and apprehension. It was eight-
thirty. She'd be home by nine. Maybe.

The lights of town faded as she walked. The cold of
the pavement seeped into her feet, leaving them numb.
The bonus was that they no longer hurt. Her hands
burned. Her face ached from the cold and from clench-
ing her jaw.

Ten minutes into the walk, her whole body ached
from shivering. She kept trudging on in the dark.

Headlights flashed, coming toward her. She kept
walking. The truck slowed as it drew nearer. She sighed

as it came to a halt next to her. The door flew open and Gage jumped out.

"What in the world are you doing?"

She looked up at him, teeth chattering. "Walking."

"Layla, why in the world didn't you call?"

"I don't have a cell phone."

"Someone in town would have let you use their phone. Or given you a ride."

"Probably, but I didn't want to bother anyone. Besides, it isn't that far. I've walked it before. Do we have to stand here and talk?"

He opened the passenger door of the truck. "Get in."

She didn't argue. She climbed into the truck, moving the vents so they blew directly at her. The warmth seeped back into her body. Gage got in and headed to her place.

Two minutes later they pulled into her drive. "It wouldn't have taken me long."

Gage didn't answer. He got out and walked around to her side of the truck to pull the door open. "No, just long enough to freeze. Or get hit and left on the side of the road. Or abducted."

"I never realized you were such an optimist." She looked up at him, fighting the sting of tears. The heat had thawed her body and her nose. It had also obviously thawed her emotions. She sniffled and walked past him.

He didn't leave. Of course he didn't. He followed her to the house, marching up the steps of her tiny front porch and pulling the door open.

"Where were you?" he asked as he followed her in.

She kicked off her shoes and limped through the living room. "Working for Vera. Now I need to put on boots and head to the barn."

"Brandon took care of the chores."

She swallowed a lump of emotion and kept walking. She couldn't stand there and look at him, not when she felt raw, and he looked like a man ready to hug a woman. She had to pull herself together. A cup of tea. She needed tea. Ginger tea. It would settle her nerves and her stomach.

Gage didn't take the hint. He followed her into her tiny kitchen, where he seemed too tall and took up too much space.

"Where's Brandon?" The house was too quiet.

"In his room. He has homework."

She didn't know what to say. To fill the void, she reached into the cabinet and pulled out two cups. "Do you want tea?"

"Let me do it." He took the cup from her hand, their fingers brushing in the process. It was a simple gesture, she told herself. She'd touched plenty of hands today. Making change. Taking menus from customers. It didn't mean anything.

Until now, when he looked down at her, his gaze soft and far too understanding.

"I really can take care of myself."

"I know you can." He said it like he meant it. "But sometimes you could let people help."

"Gage, this goes above and beyond. It was a long time ago. It wasn't the end of the world for me. It was a lesson learned. And it didn't work out that great for you, either, did it? Cheryl never really liked you."

He laughed and took the cup, pouring cold water in it and putting it in the microwave. "Sit down. And thank you for reminding me."

"It's the truth. And you've done enough. You fixed

my fence. You've helped my brother. The debt is paid. Your conscience should be cleared. Go rebuild that chicken pen for Jack Morris."

To her delight he turned a little pink beneath his tan. "I didn't think fireworks would set the thing on fire."

"You were very bad."

He was rummaging in her cabinet. She watched him as she sat down at the table.

"What are you doing?" she finally asked. The timer on the microwave beeped. He took out the cup and dropped a tea bag into the water.

And then he went back to rummaging. He found an aluminum roasting pan she'd bought to cook a turkey and turned on the hot water. Next he pulled out a gallon pitcher. She didn't know what to say.

What could she say when he set the pan down in front of her and filled it with warm water. He went back to the cabinet and found salt. Really, salt?

She still couldn't comment. He brought her tea. He brought a towel from the drawer and then he pointed to the pan.

"What are you doing?" she asked again.

"You're soaking your feet."

Heat climbed into her cheeks as she stared at him and then at the pan of water. He pointed and she couldn't move. Gage sighed.

"I can't kneel." He pointed to the brace on his leg, "Or I would put your feet in the water for you. As it is, you're going to have to do this. But I promise you'll feel a lot better."

Her eyes filled with tears that she couldn't blink away.

Gage dropped the towel on the table and for a long

minute he stared at her as tears rolled down her cheeks. After a heart-stopping moment he leaned. His hand brushed her cheek, and then gently swiped away a tear that trickled down. She wanted to say his name, but couldn't.

She should have told him to stop. But her heart wouldn't let her. Her poor, lonely heart.

When he leaned in close, she held her breath. Her eyes closed while hot tears traced a path down her still-frozen cheeks. His lips touched hers, salty from her tears. Somehow, her hands moved from her lap to his neck. Her fingers twirled in the soft strands of hair at his collar.

His lips continued to move over hers, whisper-soft, then moved to her cheek, and then her ear. She heard him whisper her name as he leaned, still cupping her cheek in his hand.

"Now," he whispered, "put your feet in the water before it gets cold and I have to start all over again."

She nodded and moved her feet. She looked up. Gage had straightened, but he was still standing close. He picked up the cup of tea and placed it in her hands.

"I should go," he said.

She blinked a few times at the announcement.

"Okay."

He brushed a hand through hair that just moments earlier she'd had her hands tangled in. Soft hair. And he smelled good, like soap, spices and lime.

She probably smelled like fried chicken.

Of course he wanted to leave. He was Gage Cooper and she was Layla Silver, the girl who had believed him when he said they were friends. But she had believed her heart more when it said that Gage could be more than a friend.

"I'll give you a ride to work in the morning and then we'll see what we can do with your truck."

"Gage, you don't have to do that."

"I know that I don't."

"Really?" She somehow managed a smile.

"Really." He leaned in, and kissed her cheek. "See you tomorrow."

After he left she sat for a long time, holding a cup of tea that had gone cold, her feet soaking in water that was no longer warm.

Gage woke up early the next morning. He had something to do but he couldn't remember what. His dad had mentioned moving cattle from one section of pasture to another. They were expecting a buyer for a couple of younger bulls they were selling off.

He sat up on the edge of the bed and reached for the brace that he was just about tired of. He'd considered going without it, but he didn't want to go through surgery again.

The alarm clock went off, playing loud country music. He slammed his hand down on the buzzer and fought the urge to go back to sleep. Then it hit him. What he had to do. He had to be at Layla's. That's what he'd been trying to remember.

How could he forget that?

And how could he forget a kiss that shouldn't have happened? Man, he was losing it. He'd meant to help Layla. Then last night, he'd thought he should take care of her. He guessed it had been a long time since someone had taken care of her.

Layla Silver was about the sweetest woman he'd ever met. If a guy was so inclined, she'd be the kind he wanted to marry. But she deserved better than a guy who was just passing through.

He guessed his mom was right, all the times she'd told him he'd grow up and start to think about other people. She had faith in him. He smiled as he walked down the stairs and headed for the kitchen. It was barely six in the morning, but he could hear her moving around, humming softly. "Amazing Grace." He smiled, because some things never changed, and he was glad.

"Morning, Gage." She poured two cups of coffee and handed him one as he walked into the kitchen. "Sleep good?"

"Yeah, better than I deserve." He took the coffee and grabbed a slice of toast off the plate.

"I can make eggs."

"No, toast is fine. I need to run."

"Where are you going so early?"

Did he tell her the truth or pretend he didn't hear? He smiled, knowing how that would end for him. He couldn't even avoid looking at her.

"I'm taking Layla to work. I found her walking home last night, half-frozen. Her truck wouldn't start."

"She's never been good at asking for help." His mom shook her head. "I think she learned at an early age to keep things to herself."

"I guess she did." He downed his coffee, because he needed to go and he knew where this conversation was heading.

"Gage, be careful."

Yep, there it went. "I'm careful, Mom."

"Honey, you can charm apples off a tree without trying. Layla is vulnerable. She's been taking care of herself and Brandon for so long, and there you are, helping. She might get the wrong idea."

"I don't think she will. I think Layla has the right idea. She'd prefer to keep me out of her life." But he remembered that kiss last night. It didn't take much to realize he might be the one getting wrong ideas.

He turned to look out the window, because his mom had a way of seeing things. She knew how to read her kids, their expressions, their body language. She sometimes knew them better than they knew themselves.

What would she see if she got a good look in his eyes? He had to get out of the kitchen before she got too close. Or asked questions that made him think more than he wanted to.

Avoiding her wasn't easy, though. He managed to get a thermal cup, fill it with coffee and grab another slice of toast as he headed for the door.

"Later, Mom."

"You be careful." Being the woman she was, she laughed as he hightailed it out of the house.

Chapter Eight

Layla worked her second shift at the Mad Cow Tuesday evening. It had been a long, long day. Gage had shown up early that morning, helping her feed and making sure Brandon got on the school bus. She'd put an end to him catching a ride with friends. He'd skipped too many days, and the school was threatening action because he had gone over the allotted number of days a student could be absent.

How had she not known that?

As she finished cleaning her workstation at the diner, thoughts were swirling around in her head. What if he'd been better off with foster parents? It was probably too late to be questioning the judge who had given a nineteen-year-old custody of an eight-year-old.

"Hey, you look like you're carrying the weight of the world on your shoulders tonight." Vera walked up behind her, placing a hand on her shoulder as she talked. "Try to get some rest and enjoy your day off tomorrow."

"I'll try."

"You need to take care of yourself, Layla. Vera's

orders. Sleep." Vera patted her shoulder. "And if you need to talk, I'm here."

Layla nodded and finished wiping down the workstation.

Vera frowned. "You do realize, don't you, that you're not giving God the chance to help you through this."

"I'm sorry?" She blinked, trying to focus.

"Layla, honey, I know you pray. I know you believe that God can and will help you through all situations. But I also know that you think Layla Silver is a rock unto herself. And when you think that way, then you aren't trusting the solid rock."

Ouch.

Vera gave her a quick hug. "Honey, let God help. And accept the help of the people He brings into your life."

"It should be getting easier, Vera. But it isn't."

Vera stood there for a minute watching her clean. And then she put a hand over Layla's, stopping her. Layla looked up, meeting the kindness in Vera's dark eyes.

"Layla, I knew your folks from the time we were all little kids in Dawson. I knew your dad and his bad habits. I knew the bruises he put on your mama. And I know that she was a private person and taught you to be one. But there's no shame in asking for help. Your mama should have taught you that."

Layla nodded, and looked away. A wave of heartache swept over her. Vera didn't push. She took her hand off Layla's and waited.

"She never wanted people to know."

"But they knew. They just didn't know how to help.

But they would have if she'd asked. And now I'm telling you, people want to help you, too."

"Thanks, Vera."

"Are you thanking me for that good advice?" Vera smiled big. "Or are you thanking me so I'll stop talking?"

She stored lettuce in the cooler and closed the sliding door slowly, trying to find the right answer "I'm thanking you for the good advice."

"That's good, because I just saw Gage drive your truck over from the feed store. He must have gotten it running for you."

She tried but couldn't stifle a groan. "Is he still out there?"

"No, he hopped in with Jackson. I imagine he left the keys in it. Don't let that Gage Cooper get under your skin."

Layla smiled. "I won't."

A short time later she left the café. There was a note on the seat of her truck telling her to pick Brandon up at Cooper Creek. She started her truck and gave it a few minutes to warm up before taking off.

When she pulled up to Cooper Creek Ranch, lights were blazing in the barn. There were several trucks lined up in the driveway. Whoops and hollers greeted her as she stepped out of her truck. She heard the clank of metal gates and the low moo of bulls, making it pretty obvious: they were bucking bulls.

It didn't take much to know that her brother was on the back of a bull. She walked into the stable, past stalls of quarter horses worth more than her house. She headed toward the arena, and when she got to the gate she stopped to watch.

Gage stood on the back of a chute, leaning over her brother. He was pulling the bull rope for Brandon. At least Brandon wore a helmet this time. Travis stood in the arena. He saw her, then shouted something to Gage.

A few others looked her way. She saw a couple of neighbor boys as well as Wyatt Johnson, pastor of the Dawson Community Church. He was probably there for a reason. When Gage got an idea, he sure didn't let go.

Later she would probably thank him for that.

She walked through the gate and around behind the chutes as her brother spun out into the arena on the back of a big, gray bull. She continued watching as she headed for the risers where a small crowd watched the action, clapping and cheering for the riders.

Gage caught up with her as Brandon went off the side of the bull, scrambling to get on his feet and then running like crazy while Travis distracted the one-ton animal and kept it from running her little brother into the ground.

"He's doing great." Gage offered as he walked next to her.

"I'm sure he is." She took a deep breath, released it and looked at the man who had taken care of her last night. He'd run hot water for her to soak her feet. He'd made her a cup of tea. He'd kissed her until she couldn't think straight.

Now it was as if none of it had ever happened. How did he do that?

"Did your truck run okay?"

She nodded. "Yes, thank you. That's what I'd meant to say, but I got sidetracked, watching my little brother on the back of a bull. Not a steer."

Gage flashed that famous Cooper grin. "Yeah, that would kind of leave you speechless."

"I need to get him and go home."

"The two of us took care of feeding. Hey, why don't we trailer that mare of yours out here tomorrow and ride her in the arena?"

"Why?"

He shrugged. "No reason. I know you're working her, and that's hard to do in this weather."

"I don't know, Gage." She glanced back to the arena, to the next kid sitting on a bull. Jackson was pulling the bull rope as the boy tried to get his seat on an animal that seemed pretty intent on getting him off before the gate even opened. "You should go help Jackson."

"Think about my offer." He shot her another grin that made her knees go weak.

"I will." No. She wouldn't think about it. She couldn't.

Gage touched her arm, then leaned in close. "Let yourself have fun."

His breath fanned her cheek and he smelled so good, like leather and the outdoors. Have fun, he said? She couldn't remember the last time she'd really gone out and had fun. She didn't have the time or money for fun. She didn't have the energy.

"Gage, I don't..."

He grinned. "What...? Have fun?"

"I'd love to have fun. I don't have the time." She saw his smile fade. "Look, I'm not trying to make you feel bad. I just want you to understand."

"I do understand. I know that you work hard. I also know that you need a break."

She glanced around, making sure they didn't have

an audience. Everyone else seemed focused on the bulls and the riders. "You have no idea what my life is like. You can take off at the drop of a hat. You can buy a horse, sell a bull, or travel to Colorado for a rodeo. I have to make sure the electric bill gets paid, that there is food for a kid that eats more in a day than I do in a week and outgrows his shoes every month. I have to make a payment or…"

She stopped because she'd said too much. Gage didn't need to know her reality. It wasn't his fault that their lives were worlds apart.

"Make a payment or what?" Gage's hazel eyes locked with hers, looking ten years older. Of course he would zero in on that part of the conversation.

"Nothing. Listen, I have to go. Can you bring Brandon home later? He has school tomorrow, so he can't stay out late."

Gage nodded slowly, but his smile didn't return. "I'll bring him home."

"Thanks."

She started to walk away but he caught up with her. He walked with her out the side door, into the cold night. She looked up at a sky with millions of stars sparkling like diamonds in the velvety darkness.

"Layla, is there something I can do to help?"

She smiled up at him. "You've helped, Gage. You fixed my fences. You've spent time with Brandon. Really, you don't have to keep this up."

"I know."

"Okay, then it's over now. I'm sure there are other people on your list."

She had to say the words because it was the only way

she could protect her heart from him, from the soft look in his eyes and the gentleness that changed everything.

"There are definitely other people on my list. But I'm committed here. Not just to you, but to Brandon."

"But what happens to Brandon when you leave?"

"I'll make sure there are people who will spend time with him. If you'll let them. You have to admit, you haven't actually invited people into your life."

"I know." She sighed at the words that mirrored Vera's and looked away, watching as lights came on in the Cooper home. A dog barked in the distance. "I should have asked for help."

"Now you have help."

"Right."

"I'll be over in the morning with the trailer." His smile came back full force as he spoke. She should tell him no. It was easy to let him be in Brandon's life. But in hers?

She stood there looking at him, waiting for the words to form. What was it about him that tied her tongue in knots?

Brandon watched the play of emotions that flickered across Layla's always-expressive face. He should have let it go and not pushed her. She'd given him an out. But the truth was he didn't want an out. Nope, he wanted to be in her life.

He couldn't kiss her again, though. A kiss implied something. It connected two people. And connections were not his thing.

But standing there in the moonlight with her, he thought maybe there was a connection. He wanted to pull her close, bury his nose in her hair, then kiss her until they both forgot how cold they were.

"I have too much to do, Gage."

He smiled at her objection. It sounded familiar. She was still the good girl. He was still the bad boy asking her to skip school. Back then she had informed him, in all seriousness, that she didn't have a 4.0 grade point average by accident. She wasn't going to blow it on a day of random fun.

He laughed, remembering, and she shot him that same serious look that she'd given him years ago. Back when he'd considered that she might be prettier than her friend Cheryl, if only she'd smile more.

"What's so funny?" she asked, looking a little peevish, like a librarian dealing with rowdy students.

"Nothing, just that you've told me that before. And I still don't buy it. You need to have some fun, Layla. You need to laugh and relax."

Tears filled her dark eyes. "I don't have time to relax."

"Tomorrow you're going to make time. I'll be over early to help with chores and then we'll bring that mare over here for a real workout."

"I have laundry and housework."

"Those things can wait. A sixty-degree day in December shouldn't be wasted." He winked, hoping to seal the deal. "We'll hang out, have lunch, be friends and maybe share secrets."

A smile reappeared on Layla's face, and he felt pretty happy that he'd been the one to put it there. Yeah, he could make people smile, but this was different. He hadn't known many people who needed to smile the way she did.

Man, he didn't know many people whose smile he needed as badly as he needed hers.

"Be friends?" She continued to smile. "You can tell me who you want to marry."

"I'm afraid to report that's a pretty short list, so we'll have to move on to my favorite color."

"What is your favorite color?" she surprised him by asking.

"Brown." He tucked a strand of hair behind her ear. "Light brown with streaks of blond."

She was still smiling. And he wanted to keep that smile on her face. In that moment he wanted her smile more than he wanted a ninety-point ride on a bull that had never been covered for eight seconds.

"That smile looks good on you." It was the corniest line he'd ever uttered, and of course she didn't fall for it.

"I'm leaving now." She pulled her keys out of her pocket.

"Oh, come on, I didn't mean it."

She opened the truck door, then shot him a look. "So you don't like my smile?"

"Of course I do, but I didn't mean to sound like an actor in a romantic comedy."

She stood on the running board of her truck. Somehow her hand held his. He didn't know how that had happened. To his surprise, she pulled him close, leaning to kiss his cheek. "Thank you."

She closed the door and started the truck with no problems. The engine didn't sound good, but at least it was working. A new engine, a new transmission, the list for that old truck went on and on.

She waved and drove off. As she went past the house,

the dog ran out of its doghouse and followed along behind her. Gage headed back to the barn.

The guys were putting the bulls back in the pen. Brandon was sitting on the risers, an ice pack on his cheek. Gage walked around the chutes to where Layla's little brother sat, blinking against the sting. He pulled the ice pack off the kid's cheek and flinched.

"Oh, she is going to be mad at you." Gage grinned at Brandon. The kid shot him a dirty look.

"She's going to be more mad at you."

"I was outside. This can't be my problem."

Brandon stood up. The kid was almost as tall as Gage, and standing like he meant to throttle him. "Gage, I think you're great, but don't mess with my sister."

"I'm not going to mess with your sister, Brandon. I'm trying to help her out a little." Gage meant to walk away but he stopped. "You have to admit, things haven't been easy for her."

"I guess not." Brandon walked alongside him as they headed out of the barn. "She worries a lot."

"I know she does." Gage pushed the door open and motioned Brandon out ahead of him. "You could make it easier for her, you know."

"Yeah, I guess."

"You guess?"

At the truck, Brandon shrugged. "I don't know why you care all of a sudden."

He hadn't thought about it but she made it easy to care about her. Maybe because she was so determined to do everything on her own. Maybe because something happened in his gut when he made her smile.

"Well?" Brandon climbed in the truck and shot Gage a look.

"Well, what?" Avoidance was his greatest gift. He knew how to avoid conversations and avoid relationships in equal measure.

"Do you like my sister?"

"I'm not sixteen, Brandon."

"What's that got to do with anything?" The kid didn't look like he meant to give this up anytime soon.

"Brandon, I'm a grown man and I'm not worried about finding a girl to wear my class ring."

"They don't do that anymore."

"Really?"

"Yeah, really. And my sister sure isn't going to wear any ring of yours."

Gage nearly choked. He hadn't been planning on giving her a ring. Any kind of ring. And he sure hoped Granny Myrna didn't have any more heirloom rings stashed away somewhere. Statements like Brandon's made him want to pack his bags and head out sooner than later.

It would have been easy to do, but he'd made promises and he wasn't going anywhere until he knew he'd settled things with Layla.

Chapter Nine

The sky was dusky gray, and frost covered the ground when Layla walked out to the barn Wednesday morning. She exhaled and her breath turned to steam in the cold air. It was cold for early December, but the weather was supposed to break soon. The forecast said it would be close to sixty, then for the rest of the week it would be back to normal temperatures. That meant cold again.

She didn't mind a brisk morning and frosty grass crunching under her feet. When she walked through the doors of the barn, her mare greeted her with a soft whinny.

"Hey, Pretty Girl, I'm glad to see you, too." Layla brushed aside the thought of selling the mare. She didn't want to think about it. Not yet. She loved the bay with her refined head and the beautiful gait that caused cars to slow down and watch when she pranced through the field.

Layla tossed a flake of hay into the metal rack and headed to the feed room for grain. The dog barked. She walked out, almost expecting Gage. Instead she found her brother, tall and awkward with his dark hair un-brushed and his eyes still half-sleepy.

"You'd best get ready for school."

He pinched the cloth of the dark blue hoodie he wore and shrugged. "I'm ready.

"Oh." She didn't know what else to say.

"I thought I'd help you feed."

"Okay. Well, can you grab a bag of grain and feed the cows."

"Sure." He trudged into the feed room and walked back out with a bag of grain. "What about hay?"

"I put a bale out two days ago. They should be fine for now."

The big round bales would last her small herd quite a while. And since the price of hay had gone up during the drought, that was a good thing.

Brandon hefted the bag of grain to his shoulder and walked out of the barn. She watched him open the gate and head for the feed trough. Her little brother, will-ing to help. Without being asked. She didn't know how to process the turn of events, but she wasn't going to question it.

A few minutes later Brandon returned. He brushed a hand through his hair. "Got it. I put the bag in the burn barrel."

"Okay."

"Is that all you can say?" Back to moody teen voice.

"No, it isn't. Thank you for helping."

He shrugged again. "Yeah, well, I gotta go. The bus will be here."

"Right, the bus."

He started down the drive, but he stopped. She

waited, and he turned back around. "Hey, I'm sorry that I've been such a pain."

"It's okay."

He shrugged and took off, walking fast because the bus was coming over the hill and would stop at the end of their drive in about two minutes. As great as his help had been, she didn't trust him completely. She stood in the opening of the barn, watching until he got on the bus.

"Pretty Girl, I don't know what to make of that, but I think we have Gage Cooper to thank." It pained her to admit it, even to a horse.

The horse reached, nibbling at the sleeve of her coat. Layla pulled a carrot out of her pocket.

"You always expect a treat, don't you?"

The mare ate the carrot in three bites, nodding her head up and down as she chewed. A truck lumbered up the driveway, the diesel engine distinct. She peeked out the open double door of the barn, knowing it would be Gage.

"Great, he didn't give me time to find an excuse to turn him down."

The mare stared, finishing the last bite of carrot and then dropping her head to nibble at the pieces that had fallen on the ground. The truck door slammed shut, and the horse's head came back up as her ears twitched and she whinnied.

"Don't greet him like you're glad to see him. It'll go to his head."

"Is that what you think of me?" Gage walked through the door of the barn, a cowboy in a heavy canvas jacket and his hat pulled low. He had shaved, and she could see where he'd nicked his chin. The clean scent of his aftershave still clung to his skin.

"I guess you're not terrible," she conceded, and of course he smiled.

He walked up to the stall door, admiring her horse. "Layla, you can't sell this horse."

"I don't know if I have a choice."

"If you need money, I can loan…"

She held up her hand to stop him. "No, you can't. I'm not going to borrow money from you. I'm going to make it through this. I've made it all these years, and I'm not giving up now."

"But this horse is special."

"She's just a horse." Layla said the words, wishing she meant them. If it had been any other horse, maybe. But this horse, she *was* special. It showed in her deep brown eyes, in the way she interacted with people. She wasn't just any old horse. Layla's eyes stung, and she blinked away the moisture before turning to Gage with what she hoped looked like an easy smile.

"Right, just a horse." Gage shook his head. "And elephants fly."

"There was that Dumbo character."

"Yeah, sure." He tossed her a lead rope that she'd left hanging on a hook. "Let's go."

"Go?"

"To the ranch."

"I have to clean house and do laundry. This is my only day off."

"You have to have some fun."

"I can't, Gage. In your world, the clothes will get washed and the house gets cleaned while you're in the barn with the bulls or the horses. In my world, I do those things."

"I can do those things."

"I'm sure you probably can."

"Okay, let's go." He reached for her hand. "I'm going to show you what a Cooper man can do."

"What does that mean?"

He leaned in close, grinning. Layla took a step back.

"It means, Miss Layla Silver, that I'll show you how well I can sweep and mop. My mom is an equal opportunity chore master. It isn't only housework for girls and farmwork for the boys. And I don't always live at home."

"Oh."

"What did you think I meant?"

"Nothing. Gage, I can clean my own house."

"And I'm going to help you." He took a step closer, narrowing the distance between them. Distance she needed in order to think clearly.

"Really?" The word came out as a whisper.

"Really. Because Cooper men are pretty amazing." He slipped a finger under her chin, and she looked up as he leaned to kiss her.

This was becoming a really bad habit, she thought as he stole her breath with that kiss. His lips were warm and gentle. He brushed them across hers, sweet, achingly sweet. Layla closed her eyes and wished she was anyone else, so that she could allow herself to fall in love with Gage Cooper.

But she wasn't anyone else. She was Layla Silver, and she knew that he played games. She knew that he loved the freedom of his life.

She pulled back, shaking her head as she put space between them. "Stop doing that."

He whistled, surprising her, because he looked as stunned as she felt. "Layla, I keep trying to stop. It isn't easy to do."

"It should be."

"If you say so." He continued to look at her, serious, unsmiling. "I promise you, I didn't plan on this."

"On what?"

He shook his head. "Never mind. Let's get that house cleaned up."

Before she could answer, he took off. She followed him across the yard to the back door of the house. He reached it first, holding it open for her. *Always the gentleman,* she thought.

She couldn't quite be sarcastic because she knew he did try very hard to be considerate. His parents had raised him right. Thinking back to high school, she realized that he had offered her friendship. He hadn't pretended to want more. She had wanted it. She had wanted him to love her.

It was an uncomfortable thought that she quickly shed as she walked into her tiny kitchen and faced the sink full of dishes and floors that needed to be mopped.

Why had she allowed him into her life this way? Back then, she'd been young, naive. Now she had no excuses. So what was her reason?

Almost two hours later, Gage dumped a bucket of dirty mop water off Layla's back porch. The border collie, Daisy, ran across the yard, barking as if he had just realized Layla had company. Gage turned back into the house, walking into the kitchen where Layla was putting kitchen towels in a drawer.

She had filled a kettle of water and placed it on the back burner of the gas cooking stove. When he walked in, the whole thing seemed a little too homey. Layla in the kitchen, her brown hair pulled back in a ponytail, a smudge of dirt on her cheek. She had put out a few Christmas decorations, including a nativity on the kitchen table.

He yanked off the yellow rubber gloves she'd given him to wear while he mopped.

Yeah, way too homey. He shuddered and shoved the bucket into the utility closet next to the fridge.

"Do you want tea?" Layla pulled two cups out of the cabinet. "And I have pumpkin muffins."

"Tea is good. I had a big breakfast."

She shrugged and dropped tea bags in the cups before filling them with the hot water from the kettle.

"Thank you for helping." She looked back at him.

"No problem." He reached for one of the cups. "You drink a lot of hot tea."

"It's comforting. My mom used to..." She looked away. "My mom made tea for me. It was her way of making things better. When I needed to talk, she would make tea. When things were... When things got bad, she made tea."

He wondered if any of those talks had been about him. Layla smiled at him, her eyes soft, like a dusky evening sky. "Yes, we discussed you."

"I wasn't going to ask."

"I know." She nodded toward the table. "Have a seat."

"Are you going to..."

She shook her head. "No, I'm not going to tell you what my mom said, or what I said to her. It wouldn't do your ego any good."

"You haven't exactly been easy on my ego."

"I don't think it will hurt you if there's one woman in the world who doesn't fall at your feet."

He grinned as he sat down. Man, she was killing him. His ego was battered, his knee ached. And yet he was still smiling. How in the world did she do that?

"We should go soon."

She looked up from her cup of tea, barely hiding a smile. "Go where?"

He pointed at her. "Ha, good try. To the ranch. As if you didn't know. I didn't clean your house for my health. I did it so you would agree to bring your horse to the ranch."

"Her name is Pretty Girl, and I don't need to take her to your place to work with her."

"We have a nice, cozy indoor arena."

"Yes, I'm aware of that." She bit down on her lip and stared at the cup she still held.

"You're tempted. I can see it in your eyes."

"Yes, I'm tempted."

"Your house is clean. You got your laundry caught up."

"Right, I know. And thank you for that. It was nice, having help."

"So let's go. Get your riding clothes on, and let's head to the ranch. You might have noticed I'm pulling a trailer."

"I noticed that you take a lot for granted."

"It's my special charm. I'm confident."

"Yes, you are." She eyed his left leg. "How will you ride?"

"It isn't that difficult. The brace gives."

"Are you supposed to ride?"

He stood, grimacing as he put weight on his leg. "I'll be fine. Go get ready and I'll load your mare."

Before she could stop him, he headed out the door. She'd either be ready when he came to get her or she'd be sitting at the table waiting to tell him she wouldn't go.

He was leading the mare into the trailer when Layla appeared in jeans, riding boots and a plaid jacket. Her white knit cap was pulled down over her head and her eyes glistened. From the cold or tears?

"Ready to go?" He stepped down from the trailer and closed the back.

"Yes." She looked from him to the horse.

"Layla?"

She nodded. "Ready."

He watched as she walked around the front of the truck and climbed in the passenger side.

Now he was starting to doubt if he was prepared for this, and he didn't know why. It was starting to feel a lot like the way a guy must feel when something was about to tie him down. He'd always imagined he wouldn't want that to happen to him.

Neither of them spoke on the way to Cooper Creek. He reached to turn up the radio. "Do you like Alan Jackson?"

"Of course."

"What about Gibson Cross?"

Cross was a country singer who owned property in Dawson but hadn't been around much in the past few years. "Yes. He helped, you know. With my parents' funerals. He put money in my account."

He hadn't expected this. Why hadn't he really known her before? They'd grown up in the same town. They'd gone to school together. She'd tutored him in chemistry and introduced him to his best friend. And he'd known little about her, other than she kept to herself and sometimes she tried to cover up bruises.

"That was good of him." He cleared his throat. "He's a good man."

"The Coopers helped, too."

He glanced her way and then back at the road. "Yeah, we're good people, too."

Silence hung between them. He didn't know what to say as he parked near the barn. Reese was getting out of Jackson's truck. Great, he needed a big dose of brotherly love the way he needed a stomach virus.

"Why did you groan?" Layla asked as she reached to open her door.

"Brothers."

"You do have some."

"They're always in a guy's business."

She laughed at that. "Which is another reason to take off to parts unknown."

"Something like that."

"You have family, Gage. Be happy about that."

Okay, suddenly he felt like a heel. He tried to smile but couldn't. "You're right."

They were unloading the mare when Jackson walked out of the barn. He whistled when he saw the mare.

"Your horse, Layla?"

She nodded. "Yes, she's mine. She's the only one I have left."

"She's nice." Jackson walked around the horse. He ran his hand over her back, nodding his appreciation.

"Thank you." Layla took the lead rope from Gage.

"We're going to work her a little."

"While you're at it, work that gray for Dad. He needs a good hour under the saddle."

"And the chestnut gelding?" Gage closed the trailer.

"Yeah, if you have time. He always tries to buck when you get him in the arena."

"Good to know." Gage opened the double doors at the end of the barn and Layla led the mare through. He watched as she tied the horse, then he went back to the truck for her bridle and saddle. He'd loaded it, knowing she would want her own tack.

When he walked back in, Reese had joined Jackson. The two were discussing Layla's mare. He was surprised she didn't try to sell the animal to Jackson. But he knew she didn't want to part with the horse. That was evident in the way she brushed the horse, spoke to it, touched it.

Something about that made him itch a little. He'd never had a hard time parting with anything. But then, he hadn't parted with anything he really cared about. Not a loved one, a favorite horse, not even his first truck. He liked his life unencumbered. He craved the open road and new places. He loved riding bulls because it kept him on the road.

It was easy. Load up the truck and go.

He could do it today if he wanted. No one would question him. But his gaze landed on Layla, and everything changed.

He told himself it was because he still had a lot of

fences that needed mending. If God really had given him another chance, he needed to make the most of it.

That's what was keeping him here. Or at least that was the story he was sticking with.

Chapter Ten

Layla slid off the back of a pretty gray mare that Gage had asked her to ride. She smiled as she reached to pat the horse's face. Super sweet. She loved the mare. She loved riding in the Cooper arena. And she had to admit, it had felt good putting her mare in one of the large stalls in the stable.

"Having fun?" Gage walked up to her, leading the gelding he'd been riding. He was limping more than usual, and she gave a pointed look at his leg. "I'm fine. And you're having a good time, so don't ruin it by lecturing."

"I think we should be done." She glanced at her watch. "It's getting late."

"It's only one o'clock." He pulled the reins of the gelding tight when the animal nudged at him. "Let's go have lunch."

"Lunch?"

"At the house." He inclined his head toward the exit. "Let's get these two brushed and turn them out to pasture."

"What about my mare?"

"She's fine in the stall. She's munching on hay and acting pretty pleased with herself."

Layla walked next to him, leading the mare, who was practically resting her head on Layla's shoulder. "I'm sure she is happy. As long as she isn't too happy here. She does have to go home with me."

"She wouldn't want to stay here. Too many men."

"When are you leaving, Gage?" she blurted out. As soon as the words left her mouth, she wanted to pull them back in.

Gage shifted to look at her. "In a hurry to get rid of me?"

"A little." She smiled as she said it, but maybe she meant it, just a little. She didn't want to get attached to him. Maybe the sooner he left, the better.

"Probably after the first of the year." He tied his gelding and flipped a stirrup over the saddle to undo the cinch. "I can't ride until the doctor releases me. Unless I decide to ignore him."

"What will you do when you get tired of riding bulls?"

He looked at her as he pulled the saddle off the horse's back. "What's this? Twenty Questions?"

"I've known you my whole life, and you've always been Gage Cooper, megaflirt and bull rider."

"Great. They should put that on my gravestone— Gage Cooper. He was a happy man."

She rolled her eyes at him. "I didn't mean it quite like that."

"I hope it'll say more than that. I'm not going to be young and immature forever."

"So what will it say?"

He shrugged. "I guess, Gage Cooper, One Good Guy."

"That's perfect."

"Thank you. I'm glad you approve. But that isn't what you mean, is it? You want to know if I'm going to grow up, get a job and settle down?"

He looked sad, just for a minute, then he wasn't. He smiled and laughed, the way he always did. But she wasn't fooled.

"Gage, you are a good person."

He led the horse to the end of the barn, opened a door and turned the animal loose, sending him off with a light swat on the rump to get him moving before he closed the door. He limped back down the aisle to where she had tied the mare she'd ridden. She looked up from brushing her.

"I'm not the good one, Layla. I'm not Reese, or even Jackson. Travis is a great husband and he'll be a great dad. I'm not the kind of guy who settles down. I always feel like I need to be moving on to the next adventure." He stepped close and brushed a strand of hair behind her ear, sending shivers down her spine. "And you are worth marrying."

Her heart quaked a little at the soft words, the soft look in his eyes. "Gage, don't."

"What do you want, Layla?"

"I want to survive raising my brother." She smiled and shrugged. "I used to want more, but life changed. There aren't many men who want to date a woman raising her younger brother. I love Brandon and I can't put him second."

"You shouldn't. But someday you should put yourself first."

She nodded. His hand was still close to her ear. He stroked her hair and then backed away.

"You asked what I want. I want to win the world title, and then I want to come home and work at Camp Hope."

"Camp Hope?" That surprised her. The camp located outside of Dawson catered to inner-city youth three weeks each summer, three weeks to low-income rural children and two weeks to military families.

"You might not know this about me, but I have a degree. I'm a test away from being a licensed social worker."

"Social worker?"

"Family services. Low pay, long hours, not a lot of glory."

Everything she had ever known about Gage Cooper changed in that moment. He became a person she had never expected.

"I'm impressed," she finally managed to say.

"Don't be. I've been out riding bulls, putting money in the bank. Other people are working the long hours and taking the grief for the job they do."

They turned the mare out to pasture and headed for the house. The day had warmed up as forecasted, close to sixty degrees. Layla slipped out of her jacket as they walked.

"What made you choose social work?"

"Natural choice, I guess." He motioned with his hand at the house, the farm. "I grew up here. I have everything. And my parents filled this house, and our lives, with kids who wouldn't have had anything if it hadn't been for my parents and their ability to love. My folks realized the important fact that love doesn't run out.

You can love one kid or a dozen, and love them all. That's pretty impressive."

Where had her fun-loving Gage Cooper gone? She looked at him, saw his face and his smile. But now she knew he had more layers than she'd ever guessed.

His hand reached for hers and she let him hold it. She squeezed back and he chuckled a little. "Don't go all soft on me, Silver."

"Why do you say that?" She lifted her chin a notch to show that she wasn't going soft.

"The look in your eyes, like you just discovered my secret. I'm still Gage. I've never had a committed relationship, other than with my family. I'm still going to leave in a month."

They kept walking.

When they entered the kitchen of his family home a few minutes later, they were greeted by Angie and Myrna Cooper. Gage hugged his grandmother and kissed his mom on the cheek. She wrinkled her nose and stepped away.

"You smell like horses."

"You married a cowboy and you still haven't gotten used to it?" Gage laughed and kissed his mom's cheek a second time. "What's for lunch?"

Layla stood off to the side watching them, wanting. She shook her head to break free from what she wanted. Family. She'd never wanted family more than she did right now. She wanted it for herself and for Brandon. She wanted a house that looked and smelled like Christmas.

There was even a little tree on the counter, a tiny tree with tiny decorations.

"Layla, I bet you're starving." Myrna Cooper motioned her into the room. "Don't let Gage keep you in the barn, honey."

"Oh, I didn't mind. It was wonderful."

Myrna's brows arched, and she looked from Layla to Gage. "Was it really now?"

Gage shot his grandmother a look. Then he grabbed a pitcher out of the fridge.

"Tea?" he asked.

"Please."

As he poured, his mom pulled lunch meat from the fridge, then cheese, mayo and a bowl of grapes. "Layla, do you like smoked turkey?"

"Yes, thank you." Layla eyed the sink. "May I wash my hands?"

"Of course. While you do that, I'll make your sandwich."

Layla turned as Angie pulled slices of bread from the loaf and put them on plates. "I can do that."

Angie looked up from making the sandwiches. "Of course you can, but I don't mind. Relax, Layla. You deserve a day off."

A day off. She tried to remember the last time she'd had such a thing. Then Gage was at her side, sharing the sink. He was responsible for today, for the way she felt relaxed for the first time in so long. He had helped her to forget the harsh realities of her life.

As they sat down to eat, Gage's phone rang. He got up and left the table. Myrna Cooper started a conversation about Christmas plans. Layla listened as she continued eating. They talked about the meal, gift giving, who would be there and who wouldn't.

"Layla, why don't you and Brandon join us this year?" Angie asked, repeating an invitation she'd offered more than once before. "I know you think it would be too much, but with this crowd, I promise two more people won't put us over the limit."

Both ladies were looking at her, waiting. She considered it. But the idea of being surrounded by their family on Christmas Day seemed like too much.

Angie patted her arm. "You know, we're all family in God's eyes. Besides, we would love to have you with us."

"I'll think about it." She was still unsure, but knew Brandon deserved some Christmas memories that included more than the two of them eating turkey and watching old movies.

"That settles it, then." Myrna Cooper clapped her hands together, then she was off on the topic of rings. She showed Layla the engagement ring from her fiancé Winston. As she held her hand up, the light caught the brilliant gem and it sparkled.

"We plan on being married in May, Winston and I. I hope there are more weddings this summer. There's nothing like a good wedding to keep a community alive."

"Myrna." Angie shook her head.

Layla looked from one woman to the other. They were giving each other looks, and Myrna seemed far too pleased with herself. Layla felt a bit apprehensive because everyone knew Myrna loved to involve herself in the lives of her grandchildren. Especially their love lives.

"I love diamonds." Myrna positively glowed as she looked at her ring. "Are you a diamond kind of girl, Layla? Or maybe you favor pearls. Yes, I think that's it."

"Pearls are very pretty."

Gage walked back into the kitchen. "Layla, don't answer her."

"You okay, Gage?" His mother stood, her smile dissolving into a frown.

"I'm fine. Layla, that was Slade. We need to leave."

Her heart thumped hard, and she stared up at him, searching for more information.

"Gage, tell her what's wrong. Can't you see you're scaring her?"

Yes, Layla thought, she was scared. Her legs were weak and she couldn't breathe. Gage closed his eyes just briefly.

"I'm sorry. Layla, Brandon skipped school today. He's fine, but they were in an accident. Ran a truck through a fence. Slade has them out at the Tuckers fixing the fence, and Mr. Tucker said he won't press charges."

"Why did he call you?" Layla's voice shook. She didn't want to be shaky. She had to be strong. This was her life, her brother and her responsibility.

"Layla, you don't have a cell phone." His voice was rational. Reasonable. And too soft. The way it would be if he was talking to someone about to lose it.

"But he's okay?"

"He's fine."

She carried her paper plate to the trash, put her glass in the sink and turned, trying desperately to hold back her tears. Seven-year-old memories rushed to the surface. Angie Cooper put an arm around her shoulder.

"He's okay," Angie whispered, holding her close.

"I know." She fought for a deep breath. "I know." But in that moment, it reminded her too much of that night.

* * *

Gage had missed it, that panic, that fear. He shouldn't have. He should have remembered that not that long ago a trooper had asked Gage's parents to go with him to Tulsa to break the news to Layla.

"I'm sorry." He reached for the hat he'd dropped on the counter. "I should have done that differently."

"It's okay." She sucked in a breath, and he could tell she was pulling herself together. "Let's go. I can drive my truck, if you have other things to do."

"I don't have anything else to do."

"What about my mare?"

"She's fine in the barn."

She nodded, turning to Angie and Myrna Cooper. "Thank you for lunch."

"You're so welcome, Layla. And don't forget about Christmas."

They were walking out the front door when it dawned on Gage. His mom had invited Layla to Christmas at Cooper Creek. He was used to his grandmother meddling in the romantic lives of his siblings, but his mom usually stayed out of it. Or at least gave the appearance of it.

"Gage, you really don't have to drive me."

"I know that, but I want to."

She nodded but continued to stare out the window as they drove. "He's a good kid. I didn't have problems with him until the past year or so."

"He's a teenager, Layla. He needs a man to give him a little guidance."

"I know." Her voice was soft. He reached for her hand and she clasped his fingers tight. "It's my fault. I grew up keeping people out, and then when I needed them, I didn't know how to let them help."

"Old habits are hard to shake."

She smiled at him, finally. He thought about that smile, then decided it was better if he didn't. When they pulled up to the scene of the accident, the old truck driven by Brandon's buddy was sitting in the field. Brandon was busy pounding fence posts back into the ground.

"I want more for him than this. I just hope he wants more."

A dozen thoughts ran through Gage's mind, about growing up, realizing a person wanted more out of life. But he didn't know how to express it so it made sense.

"He'll grow up." That's all he said as he got out of the truck.

Brandon glanced their way as he pounded another fence post. He finished and swiped at his brow. Layla just stood there looking at him. To Gage she looked half mad, half brokenhearted.

"Layla, I know I messed up." Brandon pulled his ball cap a little lower on his dark head. He shrugged in his hoodie and looked to Gage. "I should have known better."

Layla sighed. "You *do* know better."

"Yeah, I do." He looked down at the ground and then at his sister. "I'm sorry."

"I know you are. But there are consequences." She looked from Gage to Slade to Brandon. "I think you'll have to stop riding bulls."

"But…" Gage said at the same time as Brandon.

Layla silenced them both with a look. "For the next month, no bulls. Brandon can do chores for Mr. Tucker, and he can continue to work at Cooper Creek. He can't go anywhere with Jason."

Jason, Brandon's friend, looked a little sheepish. Gage wondered where his folks were.

"Fine." Brandon went back to pounding posts.

"Seems to me you're getting off pretty easy, Brandon." Slade McKennon, soon to be Gage's brother-in-law, had that voice of authority Gage admired. Both of the boys lowered their heads and kept on working.

Brandon said, "Yes, sir."

It took another hour for them to get the fence repaired. Jason got in his truck and headed across the field to a gate. Brandon turned to look at Layla.

"Get in Gage's truck. He'll give us a ride home." She walked up to Mr. Tucker. "He's all yours. Any chores you need done, you let him know. I'll have him get off the bus here, if that's okay with you."

Mr. Tucker nodded and looked at the teenager. "After he's done, I can give him a ride home. Or to Cooper Creek. Mondays and Thursdays I can use some help. Those chicken houses I've got take a lot of my time. My wife has been on me to take her to dinner once in a while. Brandon can help me get work done and that'll keep the missus happy."

"Thank you, Mr. Tucker. If there are any other expenses, just let me know." Layla slowly trudged along the fence line to Gage's truck.

Gage followed them to his truck, knowing full well that Layla couldn't afford to have any other expenses piled on top of the ones she already had.

Brandon had to know that. So why did the kid keep getting himself into trouble?

Gage climbed in his truck. Layla sat in the middle

between him and her brother. That meant the whole ride back to her place, their shoulders touched and her sweet scent teased. He had more troubles than Brandon Silver ever dreamed of.

Chapter Eleven

Friday night at Vera's started out busy, but then the Mad Cow cleared out. The sky looked iffy, and people were worried about sleet. Layla looked out the window at the light coating of white sleet already covering the sidewalk. A block down from the Mad Cow, headlights flashed on the road. It looked a lot like Gage's truck.

She hadn't seen him for a few days, not since the day after Brandon's accident. Gage seemed to have gotten it when she told him he no longer owed her anything. The day after Brandon's accident, Gage had brought her mare back, unloading a dozen bales of good hay with the horse. And then he'd left, telling her he had to drive livestock to an auction outside of Tulsa.

"Do you want to help me decorate the tree?" Vera asked, walking up behind her.

Layla smiled at Vera's reflection in the window. "Of course."

"Have you put a tree up yet?"

"Not yet. Maybe next weekend."

"It's only a few weeks till Christmas."

"I know." Layla spied the box with Vera's tree. "Let's decorate."

"Layla, why don't you kids spend Christmas with me and my family?"

"We're fine, Vera. The Coopers invited us over."

"Then you should go. Honey, they won't notice two more. The more the merrier on Christmas."

"Thanks, Vera. I'll think about it."

Vera's dark brows arched. "No, you won't."

With a smile and a little chuckle, Layla started to put up the tree. And while she worked, Vera set up her nativity collections. She had several. She bought them in different parts of the country, and she loved them.

Vera loved Christmas. She overdecorated every year with tinsel, garland, glittery decorations and lights. Soon the inside of the Mad Cow would look like Christmas had exploded all over the small café.

But it was more than the beautiful decorations. Vera loved Christmas because she loved Jesus. Every day, every hour, she lived her faith. Over the years Layla and others in the community had been touched by that strong faith.

Vera walked away from the nativity on the counter by the register. She peeked out the window and shook her head. "That sleet is coming down pretty hard. You should probably head on home."

"It would only take a few minutes to decorate the tree."

Vera glanced to the window and then back at the tree. "No, I'll do it in the morning. You take that extra fried chicken for you and Brandon."

"I'm not really hungry and he's probably already eaten."

"Layla, honey, you need to eat. You're pale and you're losing weight."

"I haven't felt so great this week. It'll pass. But I'll take the chicken home for Brandon."

"I'd be happier if you went to a doctor for a checkup."

Layla shook her head. "I can't."

"I know you have no insurance, but it isn't worth risking your health."

"I'll be fine in a day or two."

The sleet was really coming down. Layla shivered at the thought of driving home in the cold and snow. The heater on her truck didn't blow especially warm, and the defroster had a hard time clearing the windshield.

"Go home before the roads get slick." Vera hurried to the back and returned with containers of chicken.

"I can stay and help you close up."

"No, I can get this. And you have farther to go than I do."

Layla decided not to argue. Not only was it pointless, but Vera was right. "Thanks, Vera."

"You're welcome. And promise me that you'll stay home tomorrow if you're still feeling sick."

"I promise, but I know I'll be fine."

"Of course you'll be fine." Vera handed her the container of food. "But in case you aren't…"

"I'll call."

Vera let her out the front door and then locked it behind her. Layla hurried to her truck, sliding a little on the sleet-covered sidewalk. The sleet stung her cheeks as she ran. She cranked the truck's engine a few times and finally it roared to life. Headlights flashed through the cab. A big, blue Ford truck pulled next to her. She rolled down her window as the driver's side window on the other truck lowered.

"I just dropped Brandon off at your place and saw that you weren't home yet." Gage smiled, and something inside her relaxed.

No, she couldn't do this. Couldn't feel this. She fought for something to say, some way to dismiss him. She didn't have time for a broken heart. She didn't have the energy to stop him from storming into her life and taking over.

Gage was still talking. She blinked a few times and refocused as he said something about following her home.

"You don't have to." She could make it the short distance to her house without the truck dying. She told him so.

"I'm sure you can," he answered. "But I'm still going to follow you. I want to make sure you get home safe."

"Really, I do this every day. And you're probably ready to get home."

Gage let out a sigh. "Layla, you're just about the most stubborn woman I've ever met. You do what you want, but you can't stop me from going in the same direction as you."

And for whatever crazy reason, she smiled. And he smiled back.

"Fine, Gage, follow me home."

"Are you going to make me a cup of tea?"

"I thought you were following me, then heading on to your house?"

"Why would I do that when I'm obviously going out of my way to follow you home?"

She didn't answer. She couldn't. Instead she rolled

up her window and eased out of the parking lot with Gage a safe distance behind.

Safe? There was nothing safe about the man. And yet, she smiled all the way home.

When she pulled into her drive, he followed. He parked next to her, getting out before she did. She had to rummage in the seat for her mail, gather up the containers of chicken, grab her purse and open her door. But he had her door open and stood there, tall and broad-shouldered in his heavy coat, his face shadowy in the dark night.

"Let me carry something."

She handed him the containers of chicken.

"Thank you." She remembered her manners.

They walked up the steps together, stomping to shake the sleet off their shoes before entering the house.

"No tree?" Gage asked as they walked through the door.

"Not yet. I haven't really had time."

"I can cut you down one."

She shook her head. "Nope, we're done, Gage. You don't owe me anything. You never owed me."

"What are you talking about?" He took off his hat and raked a hand through his dark brown hair. He tossed the hat on a coffee table, as if it belonged there. As if *he* belonged.

Layla looked at that dark hat, and then back to the man standing in front of her. Once, a long time ago, he'd been a boy. A teenager with acne and a big smile. He'd loved all the girls, flirting and conquering their hearts as if he'd been a conquistador taking new lands for his country.

Now? She didn't really know him now. She didn't

know why he was standing in her living room with that puzzled half smile on his face.

"Making amends, remember?" She walked on to the kitchen. He followed, setting the chicken on the counter. He leaned against the counter, arms folded across his chest.

"Yeah, making amends." He nodded.

"You thought you owed me something. You needed to feel better about yourself. Right?" She ignored the soft smile on his lips. "You never really owed me. I haven't thought about high school and what happened since. Well, not since high school. My life has been too busy to sit around and worry about a silly game you played with..."

"With your heart." He didn't smile.

"Sure, but that was ages ago. It's over. You've been great, helping me with Brandon. He loves you, the Coopers and your ranch."

"And our bulls."

"Yes, your bulls. He thinks he'll make a great bull rider someday."

"He could. He has talent."

"Gage..." He still had the ability to undo her common sense. She definitely needed him out of her life so she could get back to her normal routine.

"When I got hit by that bull in Vegas—" he looked down at the floor "—I could have died. When I think about that, and how I'd been treating people... It made sense to me that I should right some wrongs."

"Gage, you need to deal with this. Deal with your anger toward God."

"Why do you think I'm angry with God?"

"I've seen you walk out of church mad. The night

Reese spoke about his blindness, you left. Not just the church, but Dawson."

Gage scratched the back of his neck and then, without asking, pulled cups out of the cabinet and filled them with water.

"What are you doing?"

"Making tea. Chamomile. My mother says it's very calming."

"We're going to have tea?" As if they had tea every day. She watched the cowboy in his flannel shirt and faded jeans as he limped around her kitchen.

"Where's your brother?"

"Probably in his room."

"Should you check on him?" Gage put the two cups in the microwave.

Yes, she should check on Brandon. She should do a reality check on herself, too.

Gage watched her walk out of the room, then he slumped, resting his elbows on the counter. He wasn't no old house dog, hanging his head because he couldn't find the bone buried in the backyard. He was a grown man. A grown man who was real good at skating in and out of life.

He loved being on the road. He loved getting on the back of a bull and riding until the eight-second buzzer. New places, new people, new challenges. Those were the things he loved.

As soon as they got through Christmas, maybe New Year's Eve, he'd be on the road again, shaking off the dust of this town and people who thought they knew him. Most people didn't. Not really.

But Layla, with a few sentences, had just undone

him. Man, she'd seen right to the heart of him. That scared him.

It scared him almost as much as looking into her eyes and knowing her in a way that a lot of people didn't.

He'd never gotten that close to a woman. He'd dated a lot. Women he met at rodeos. Models representing different products. Daughters of stock owners or sisters of other riders. Those were the women he went out with. They ate dinner, they laughed, maybe they kissed a little. And then he ended it.

He didn't know their favorite colors, their middle names, or their secrets. And he didn't really care to.

They didn't know him, either. They didn't know his anger or his fears. They sure didn't bring up his faith.

She had walked back into the room on silent feet, taking him by surprise. He stood straight and smiled his best charmer smile. And she didn't respond. She stood there in soft sweatpants and a long-sleeved T-shirt, bunny slippers on her feet, giving him a look that said she wasn't falling for it.

He pulled the cups out of the microwave and tossed the sopping tea bags into the trash. He stirred a little sugar into each cup and held one out for her.

"Brandon is asleep. He woke up enough to mumble that you worked him hard today." She squinted at him a little. "Something wrong?"

"Why would you think that?"

"Because you're always smiling, like you've got the whole world in the palm of your hand. But I see the anger, the sadness behind it."

"You've been watching too much *Dr. Phil*." He sat down at her rickety old table and stretched his legs out.

Here he was, sitting in her kitchen, drinking her

tea, never really thinking about getting up and leaving. Something was really wrong with that picture. Wasn't there?

"I don't have time for television." She sat down at the table across from him. "I'm talking about you, the guy who showed up in town and decided to right past wrongs, starting with my life. But that isn't going to fix what's wrong with you."

He sipped his tea, speechless.

"Gage?"

He looked at her, really looked at her. Her brown hair hung straight and long, framing her face. Her eyes were bright. And her lips… He really was losing it.

"I'm fine, Layla."

"You're not fine. What happened to Reese was a hard blow, to all of you. Especially for the brother who always looked up to him."

He sat there staring into his empty cup and then he looked at her. Was this his life now, sitting at her table, sharing tea and talking? He should go immediately, get on a bull and get in touch with his cowboy side before she had him planting flowers in her garden.

"I'm dealing with it." What else could he say to a woman digging into his life and his heart? "I'm working through it."

"Good. Because angry doesn't suit you."

He stood up, because he needed to go. He hadn't meant to stay. He'd meant to make sure she got home safely, then head to Cooper Creek. She was right—his time for making amends was over. Somehow she had turned it all around, making it all about him, his life. He hadn't seen that coming.

"I'll see you later." He carried their cups to the sink.

"Brandon said you work tomorrow. I'll pick him up in the morning."

"I'll let him know."

She stood, and followed him to the door. They stood there for a minute, his hand on the doorknob, while she leaned against the wall, looking sleepy and a little pale.

He wanted to kiss her good-night, but he held himself back.

"Layla, you're right. I was doing this for myself. But then it became something else." He reached for the coat he'd left on the coatrack. "I'm not even sure what to say except, I'd like for us to be friends."

"We can be friends."

For whatever reason, her softly spoken words made him smile. He needed her friendship in a way he couldn't explain. Maybe because she didn't mind being honest with him. If she could stay in his life, he thought he might be a better person.

But right now, he needed to say something. And he needed to leave.

"Thanks, Layla." He hugged her. It felt right. And she hugged him back.

She stood there in his arms for a moment. He kissed the top of her head. Friendship. Yeah, right. He loosened his hold and she stepped back.

"Good night, Gage."

He nodded and slipped outside, back to the cold and sleet of a December night. The icy air felt good as he hurried to his truck.

He glanced back at the house. Layla was watching, her face pressed against the rectangular window. He wondered what she could be thinking, standing there.

Maybe she was wondering when the weather would switch back to normal.

Or maybe she was thinking about him.

He laughed at the idea. Since when did women think about him when he left?

She was probably standing there wondering what the roads would be like in the morning, thoughts of him not even crossing her mind. On the other hand, he couldn't stop thinking about her. Layla Silver, strong, quiet, never giving up. She'd had it tough, but she kept on going.

All of his life he'd taken for granted everything he had. He hadn't put much effort into his career, because he hadn't really needed to. He'd always had bull riding, the ranch and wherever the road took him. It was the perfect life.

Until now.

The thought stopped him in his tracks. Sitting at the end of Layla's drive, he wondered why all of a sudden his life no longer fit. It felt like a favorite pair of boots that were suddenly too small. Man, he hated that. Breaking in a new pair of boots was never a good time.

Finding out that his life was no longer what he wanted it to be, also not good. He glanced back at Layla's little house. He couldn't see her from where he sat in his truck. Probably better that way. He needed to head home.

He needed to do a lot of thinking, figure out what in the world he was going to do next.

Chapter Twelve

Layla stood in the kitchen of the Back Street Community Center, shivering a little, wishing someone would turn up the heat.

"Are you cold?" Heather Cooper stepped close, placing a few cans of vegetables in a box next to the one Layla had filled with cereal and snack bars.

"Freezing. I keep thinking if I work faster, I'll warm up. But I've been cold all day." She'd been cold at church, at lunch and even when she'd sneaked in a nap. But it wasn't cold outside. After the sleet on Friday and the frigid temperatures Saturday, Sunday had dawned sunny and almost warm.

"Maybe you should go home?" Heather suggested in a soft voice. "We can bring Brandon home later."

"No, I'm good."

While the women and teens boxed up the food, a group, mostly men, were outside putting the finishing touches on the set for the Living Nativity.

Today was a community service day. They were boxing and delivering food to families in the Dawson community. The Dawson Community Church youth group was wrapping gifts of coloring books, crayons and other small toys. There were also hats knitted by women in the church. No way would she miss out on all this.

She already had to bow out of the Living Nativity. She usually had a small speaking part or sang in the choir. Working two jobs, she just couldn't fit it into her schedule this year.

"Brandon is enjoying himself." Heather inclined her head in the direction of the group of kids wrapping gifts.

"He wasn't thrilled with the idea until he got here and realized he might be the only guy."

He'd wanted to be outside with the men. He was a man, he'd told her, not a kid. But he'd settled into the wrapping gig when no other guys showed up to help—making him the only guy among a group of pretty girls.

She went back to filling the boxes, hoping she could avoid Myrna Cooper, who was packaging cookies. Layla picked up a few of the packages to place them in boxes.

"Layla, how have you been, honey?" Myrna handed her another package of cookies. She had failed her task of evading Myrna.

"I'm good, Mrs. Cooper."

"Call me Granny Myrna." She smiled wide and patted Layla's hand.

Oh, I couldn't, were the first words Layla thought. But she knew better than to argue with her. She nodded. Myrna continued to give her a piercing look.

"Are you feeling well, dear?"

"I'm just cold."

Myrna lifted her hand to Layla's cheek. "My goodness, you feel warm. I hope you don't have the flu."

"I don't think I do."

"Maybe Gage should drive you home."

"No, I have my truck. And really, I don't feel sick." Okay, a little nauseated, but nothing she couldn't handle.

"If you're sure." Myrna patted her cheek. "One of these days you have to think about your future, Layla. Brandon is growing up. When is it your turn?"

"My turn?"

"To be young?"

Layla smiled at Myrna. "I think that ship has sailed. I haven't felt young since..."

"Forever?" Myrna supplied the word.

"Maybe." Layla smiled again, wanting Myrna to know that it was okay. She didn't sit around bemoaning her life. She loved her brother, the farm and her community. Someday, maybe, she'd meet someone. But life wasn't all bad. She sometimes thought people assumed that because of everything that had happened, her life must be horrible and desperate. It wasn't.

It hadn't been easy, but it hadn't been horrible. There were good moments in every day. There were bad. Didn't everyone have good days and bad?

"Well, I think your day is coming." Myrna turned to wrap more cookies.

"I'm fine, Myrna."

Myrna smiled at her again. "I know you are, honey. I know. You always have been. I think that's what puzzles people. They don't understand the kind of faith it takes to tackle life the way you've had to do."

"Thank you." Layla hurried away with the cookies. They were nearly done packing the food boxes. The clock on the wall said it was five o'clock. They would have to start delivering soon.

As if on cue, Layla heard footsteps heading down the stairs. The men returning from their work outside. Angie Cooper and a few other women had put out trays of sandwiches and fruit. There was coffee and tea to drink. The workers started lining up with plates. They would eat, and then the boxes would be loaded and delivered.

Heather walked up behind her and gave her a little push toward the food line. "Get something to eat."

Layla nodded, but food was the last thing she wanted.

Getting in line behind Gage, whether Heather planned it or not, definitely wasn't what she wanted. She held back a little, trying to come up with an excuse to head in the other direction. She'd never seen herself as a coward, but today that's exactly how she felt. Two days ago she had pushed him to talk; now she wanted to avoid all conversation.

Gage turned and saw her. He smiled shyly at her.

"Better get in line, ladies, before it's all gone." He motioned them ahead of him. "Get ahead of me. I'm pretty hungry."

"He'll take it all," Heather confirmed as she moved Layla forward in the line.

She somehow ended up in front of Gage with his hands on her shoulders, keeping her in line in front of him. He leaned in, and she felt his warm breath against her ear. "Nowhere to run."

"I hadn't planned on running." She grabbed a paper plate and handed one to him, hoping to keep his hands busy.

In front of her, Heather laughed. Layla had never

been close to Heather Cooper. They were a few years apart in age. They lived in different worlds, had different friends. Heather didn't even go to church in Dawson. Although someone had told Layla that Heather was moving back to town.

Layla took half a sandwich and a handful of grapes. Gage reached for a bag of chips and dropped one on her plate, one on his own.

"I didn't want those." She looked back at him.

"You have to eat more than a half of a bologna sandwich."

"I'm not hungry."

He took the bag of chips from her plate. "Suit yourself."

And then, somehow, she ended up at a table with Gage and Heather. One on each side of her. Brandon sat across from them. Conversation buzzed. Layla got lost in her own thoughts. As Brandon talked about the kind of truck he wanted when he turned sixteen and playing baseball in the spring, she thought about the electric bill, the loan payment and Christmas.

It wouldn't do her any good to worry. Somehow she'd get through. She always did.

"We should go." Gage stood up, taking his empty plate and hers.

Layla looked up at him, trying to process what he'd said. "I'm sorry?"

"Jeremy paired you with me. We have five boxes to deliver."

She glanced around the room and spotted Gage's half brother, Jeremy Hightree. He stood next to his wife, Beth, and her brother, Jason Bradshaw. Jason held his little boy in one arm while he talked.

Layla looked away from the group and back to Gage. She always delivered boxes with Beth. She started to say something, but Gage smiled and reached for her hand.

"Come on, Layla. We have a lot of work to do and not a lot of time to get it done."

"But I always go with Beth."

"She isn't going this year. She's exhausted. In the family way, you know."

She knew, but she hadn't expected that to stop Beth. Maybe baby number two changed things for a woman.

"Stop looking so cornered. We'll have a good time handing out these boxes of food and watching little kids smile." Gage grinned at her, and when he did, she melted.

Unfortunately he knew it. His smile grew bigger. His hazel eyes sparkled with mischief, the green flecks in his eyes made more green from the sun shining through one of the small basement windows and dancing across his face.

"Let me get my coat." She headed for the closet under the stairs.

As she slipped into her coat, the men started grabbing boxes and carrying them up the stairs. Suddenly Layla felt weak and her stomach ached. She knew full well she didn't have time to get sick.

She hurried up the stairs, wrapping a scarf around her neck as she went. The boxes were being loaded into various cars and trucks. People were pairing up. She searched for Heather and didn't see her. She thought maybe she could switch partners, that maybe Heather would rescue her.

Gage waved and called to her. He was closing the

tailgate on his truck. She took a deep breath and headed his way, smiling. Because she was going to deliver boxes of food to families in need, to children in need.

She loved Christmas traditions. She wasn't going to let a virus ruin this for her. Her gaze connected with Gage's. He smiled an easy smile and she knew it wasn't about the virus. What she felt was a good case of her heart going into defense mode, trying to protect her from what it knew would happen when Gage Cooper tired of spending time with her.

Gage drove down Back Street. He and Layla had been given houses on the west side of Dawson and just outside of town. He pulled the list out of his pocket and handed it to her.

"Where do we start?"

She looked over the addresses. "I say we go to the house farthest from town and work our way back."

"You're the boss."

She laughed at that. "Go left on 1011."

"Got it." He headed west on the main road until he found the farm road she'd indicated.

He pulled into the driveway of a house that had seen better days. Smoke poured from the chimney, and as his truck came to a stop, the front door opened and a little girl peeked out. She was dressed in pajamas but wore rubber boots on her feet. Her blond hair stuck out in all directions, and as she watched them, her thumb went into her mouth.

"She comes to church on the bus." Layla spoke softly as they sat there in the warmth of his truck. "Her name is AnaLilly."

"She's a cutie."

"Yes, she is. Their mom is single. There are three kids."

"Well, let's see if we can't make their day a little brighter." He got out of his truck, aching a little on the inside as he looked at the small house with the patched-up roof, a rusted-out van sitting in the driveway and a few scraggly chickens pecking at the frozen ground.

Layla joined him at the back of the truck. He glanced her way. She looked pretty, with jeans tucked into brown boots, a pretty brown sweater and a scarf around her neck.

Gage hefted up the box and followed Layla to the front porch. The little girl had gone back inside, and the door was closed. Layla knocked.

Finally the door opened. The mom stepped out, looking way too young to have three kids. Her blond hair was pulled back in a ponytail. She smiled at them, shy and teary-eyed.

"Gabby, we brought you a few things." Layla had taken over, smiling at the young woman barely out of her teens, he guessed.

The three kids pushed around her, trying to see who had come to visit. Gage smiled down at them. A boy and two girls, all under six or seven.

The boy looked to be about five. He had his eyes on Gage's cowboy hat. Gage smiled at the kid as the mom allowed them to enter her house. He carried the box of groceries into the kitchen and put it on the counter. When he turned, the little boy was standing there, smiling up at him.

"Buddy, I think you need a cowboy hat." Gage took off his hat, his favorite, and put it on the boy's head. "There, it's all yours."

"Oh, Mr. Cooper, he can't take that hat." Gabby tried to get the hat back. "Jimmy, give him his hat."

Jimmy ran off.

"Really, I want him to have it. Every boy needs a cowboy hat."

Gabby nodded, her dark eyes overflowing with tears. "Their daddy got himself killed in Afghanistan. We wasn't married yet or nothing. It's been real hard."

"I'm sure it has."

Layla hugged Gabby. "It'll get easier, Gabby. You make sure the kids come to church next week. We're having a big Christmas dinner."

Gabby wiped at her eyes. "Thanks, Layla, I appreciate that. And this food. Thank you. My folks went off to Oklahoma City to see if they can find jobs. I guess if they do, we'll be moving down there. Until then, we're just trying to get by."

Trying to get by. Gage knew a lot of people in her shoes, just trying to get by. He cleared his throat and looked around the little house. "Is there anything else you need, Gabby?"

She laughed a shaky laugh. "A million dollars would be nice, but I haven't seen any prize patrols wandering my neighborhood."

At least she still had a sense of humor. "If you think of anything, let me know. My brothers and I are pretty good at fixing things."

"Thanks, Mr. Cooper, I'll keep that in mind. The roof had been leaking last fall, but I found some shingles and climbed up there. It's not leaking anymore."

"Well, if it should leak again, you let us know."

"We should go." Layla hugged Gabby. The three kids were circling around her, smiling big. The little blond still had her thumb in her mouth. Layla hugged them all and then hurried out the door.

Gage followed her to the truck. They were back on the road before she could speak.

"Childhood shouldn't be so tough." She covered her eyes with her hand and he heard her sniffle. "It should be about sprinklers in the summer, building snowmen in the winter."

"I'm sure Gabby does her best to make sure those kids do a few of those things." Gage kept driving, not knowing what to say, wanting to ask her the next address. He tried to peek, but she had the paper clutched in her hand.

"I know she tries, but they see her tears, they know she worries. She barely had a childhood of her own. She was a mom by the time she was seventeen."

Man. He really couldn't imagine. He was twenty-six and not sure he was ready for marriage. Kids. He'd rarely thought about having kids. But all of a sudden, the thought crossed his mind and stuck.

"Where's the next place?"

"Down the road, turn right. The Morrison house."

"Gotcha. I'll see if Jackson and Travis can help me get her house in shape. Mom might be able to get her some services she hasn't realized she's entitled to. My mom is a genius when it comes to finding resources for people."

"That would be good."

They drove about a mile. "Layla, what about your childhood?"

She smiled at him, looking amused. "It was feast or famine, happiness and chaos. My mom tried to make everything good. My dad couldn't stay sober. And when he drank, he wasn't the nicest person to be around. Sober, he could do anything."

"I'm sorry."

"Compared to what so many people are going through, I had it easy."

They pulled up to the next house. The Morrisons. He knew them. The wife had something wrong with her and couldn't work. Jeff, her husband, tried to hold down a job, but had to take time off a lot in order to take care of his wife. Good people trying hard to make it.

He guessed that people might judge them. But Gage knew how hard they tried. Last year his dad had given Jeff a job at one of their apartment complexes. He worked part-time and was allowed time off when he needed to be at home. No more getting fired, but it wasn't an easy life.

As they walked up the steps to the ranch-style house, the door opened. Jeff's daughter, almost a teenager, Gage guessed, stood in the doorway. She wore an apron and a smudge of flour on her cheek.

"Hey, Mr. Cooper, Layla." Patty Morrison smiled, motioning them inside. "What are you all doing?"

"We're delivering some Christmas boxes, and we just happen to have one for your family." Gage followed the girl to the kitchen. The room was a wreck of dirty dishes, bowls and something boiling on the stove.

Layla turned the stove down. "Are your folks home?"

Patty shook her head. "No, my mom got real sick last night, and Dad took her to the doctor this morning. They're still in Grove. I'm cooking for me and my brother."

"What are you cooking?" Layla looked in the saucepan.

"Potato soup. I'm boiling the potatoes right now."

Patty looked in the pan. "I guess I almost boiled them over. Haden was throwing a fit about something and distracted me."

Layla carried the saucepan to the sink. "Why don't you put away the things in that box that need to go in the fridge, or the freezer. And if you get me the milk, I'll help you finish up here."

Gage looked at his watch. They had several more boxes to deliver yet. But as he watched Layla help Patty Morrison, he knew they weren't going anywhere.

"Where's your brother?" He reached up to take off a hat he no longer had.

He grinned. Sure, he was going to miss that hat. But he was more than glad his hat had a new home.

"He's in the tub. He went outside and got filthy dirty."

The tub. Gage didn't do tubs. He must have looked a little green, because Layla laughed. "Don't worry, we won't make you take care of a four-year-old."

"Good thing."

Haden hopped into the kitchen wearing only a towel and a big grin. "I got a bath."

"I see that." Gage smiled at the boy.

"My mom is sick." Haden climbed on a chair and peeked in the box. "And I love cookies."

"Not until after dinner." His sister grabbed them, placing them on the counter.

"We had potato soup last night."

"I know." Patty frowned at her brother. "I don't know how to make anything else."

"Potato soup is fine." Layla poured milk in the pan. "Do you have cheese? A few slices of cheese makes it really good."

Patty opened the door of the fridge and pulled out a package of sliced cheese. "Plenty of cheese."

Gage watched as Layla stood next to the teenager, telling her something about potato soup. They sprinkled some salt and garlic into the mix and stirred again. Then Layla hugged the girl.

"Patty, you call me if your dad can't get home tonight. I'll come and get you and Haden," Layla offered as they walked to the door a few minutes later.

Gage knew her plate was full. She had Brandon, two jobs, and he knew she had bills she was struggling to pay.

Patty cried a little as they left. She hugged Layla again and promised to call. Gage slipped an arm around Layla's shoulder as they walked back to the truck.

"I think you might be the nicest person I know." He told her as he opened the truck door.

"And it took you this long to notice?" She smiled as she hopped in, and then he saw a grimace of pain.

"Are you okay?"

"Fine." She reached for the door and closed it before he could ask more questions.

He had a lot of questions, but they had more boxes to deliver and it was getting late. Fortunately the next few houses went a little faster than the first two. Two hours after they started, they were heading to Back Street again.

"Do you want to run to Grove and get a real dinner?" he offered as they pulled into the parking lot of the community center.

Layla shook her head. "No, I'm beat."

"Are you feeling all right?"

"Not great. It's probably a bug. And now I've passed

it on to everyone we've touched. I should have stayed home but I didn't really feel sick this afternoon."

"You're sure you're okay?"

"Gage, I'm fine."

He knew he wouldn't get more from her, so he let it go. He watched as she got out of his truck and walked to hers. She started it and took off, leaving him to ponder a day that might possibly have changed his life.

Because Layla Silver was surely one of the most amazing people he'd ever met.

And he didn't know what to do about it.

Four hours later, Gage's phone rang. He had dozed off watching TV and was groggy as he answered.

"Gage, this is Brandon. Layla is really sick. She didn't want me to call anyone, but I'm worried about her. I'm going to put her in the truck and drive over to your house."

Gage woke up at that. "Wait a second. Brandon, you can't drive. Give me a minute and I'll be there."

"No, I'm bringing her to you. Your mom can help her. I can't."

Gage could hear the panic in Brandon's voice. Before he could tell him to calm down the call ended.

Chapter Thirteen

Layla had tried to fight Brandon, but her brother had
been impossible. He had wrapped her in a blanket and
carried her to the truck that was already running. She
didn't complain because it was warm inside and she
hurt so badly. Her stomach kept tightening and she just
wanted to curl up on her side, the way she'd been when
he found her in the bathroom.

She drew her knees up in the seat as the truck sped
down the driveway, slid sideways as it hit the road and
then barreled toward Cooper Creek.

"Slow down. It isn't worth having an accident. And
the bumps are killing me."

"Okay, okay." Brandon slowed down. "Layla, you
have to be okay."

"I'm okay." She kept her eyes closed and prayed she
wasn't lying.

"You don't look okay." Brandon's voice was quiet,
and she wondered if he was crying. He hadn't cried
since the day they'd buried their parents.

She opened her eyes and glanced at him, seeing for
the first time the man he would become. A sob sneaked

up on her, tightening in her throat as she fought the tears. Somehow she'd done it; she had raised him. He wasn't grown, but he was getting there.

"Don't worry," she whispered.

He only nodded, his jaw clenched, his grip on the steering wheel tight.

They drove a few more minutes. "I know I've been... I've been a real pain in the..." He cleared his throat.

"Don't say it. And you are a pain, but you're my pain, and I'm not going anywhere. Could you not hit *every* bump in the road?"

"I'm sorry. And I'm going to do better. I've been praying, and I'll do whatever you want, just don't..." He choked a little. "Don't die."

"I've got food poisoning...I'm not dying. I'll be here to stay on your case and make sure you grow up to be a doctor or something."

"I'm not that smart."

"You are. Stop arguing." She grimaced as another wave of pain hit.

And then they pulled up in front of the Coopers' big house. The lights were on. Brandon had called. He'd woken them all up. Layla groaned, because this wasn't what she did. She handled things. She didn't go running to people....

The door of the truck opened and Gage leaned in. He felt her forehead, touched her cheek. And then Angie Cooper stood next to him, in a heavy jacket, her face pale in the dark night.

"Layla, can you walk to the house?"

Layla shook her head. "I can try."

"No, don't." Angie touched her cheek. "Can you tell me what's going on?"

"My stomach. Vomiting. Maybe food poisoning?" Layla drew her legs up and trembled in the cold air from the open door.

Angie Cooper moved the arm that rested on her stomach. She pushed on Layla's side and Layla had to bite back the cry. Angie whispered that she was sorry.

"Gage is going to take you to Grove. I'll call Jesse. If he isn't on duty, he can wake up and be on duty."

"Grove?" Layla shook her head. "I don't think… I don't have insurance."

"I think you need your appendix checked, honey. That isn't something you can fix with a cup of tea and time. No arguing. Brandon can stay here with us."

"But…" She tried again but Gage's hazel eyes were dark, his mouth firm and unsmiling.

"We'll take your truck. It's already warm. You ready?"

She shook her head. How could she be?

He smiled a little, and she hadn't realized how much she needed to see that smile. She reached out to touch his face, his very sweet face. She hadn't realized how much she needed him.

He climbed in behind the wheel and they took off again. It was a quicker trip to Grove than she would have liked. He kept glancing at her, his brow furrowed, his hair messy from having been woken up.

"I'm okay," she finally managed to whisper.

"Right, of course you are. You're always okay." The words came out gruff and then he sighed.

"You don't have the right to lecture me." She thought about telling him that he didn't really know her. But in the past couple of weeks he had managed to know her better than most people.

"No," he admitted, "I don't. But as stubborn as you are, I do care."

"I'm not stubborn. I'm strong."

He laughed at that. "And still arguing."

Her old truck didn't have the best shocks in the world, and it felt as if it were hitting bumps even when there were none. The few curves they rounded felt as if they were taking them at NASCAR speeds. She held on to the door handle and somehow held on to the contents of her stomach.

"I hate to sound like I'm five, but are we almost there?"

"Almost." He turned at a light and headed down the quiet road to the hospital. Instead of parking, he pulled up to the emergency room entrance.

Before Layla could blink, there were emergency personnel rushing from the hospital. Her body started to shake and her teeth chattered. The door opened and someone reached for her.

Where had Gage gone to? She searched for him, finally seeing him off to the side. He winked. She wanted to reach for his hand but couldn't.

"Layla, I'm Dr. Arnold. Dr. Cooper is on his way in, but we're going to assess your situation and run some tests." The doctor, tall, lean, with thinning hair and glasses, put a hand on her shoulder. "Can you answer some questions for me?"

She nodded, then they were moving through the halls of the E.R. and Gage was gone. She closed her eyes and answered the questions. One question made her pause, nearly made her cry; *Who is your contact person?* Did a fifteen-year-old boy count?

What would happen to Brandon if she didn't make

it through this okay? She should have thought of that. Should have decided who should take care of him if something happened to her. He was her responsibility, not the other way around.

She opened her eyes and looked around the room. "I need to go."

"I'm sorry. I can't let you do that." Jesse Cooper leaned close to her, his dark hair and dark eyes strangely familiar and comforting.

"You need to relax, Layla. I know that's hard to do when the world is spinning, but Brandon is okay. And I listed my mom as your contact person, not your brother. Okay?"

Tears filled her eyes. "I'm sorry."

He shook his head and handed her a tissue. "Don't be. You've had a rough night. And unfortunately you're going to have a rough few days. We'll be doing some tests, and then I have a feeling you're in for surgery."

"I can't. I don't have insurance."

"That's something we'll worry about later."

"But I have to worry about it now. I can barely…" She shook her head. "Never mind."

"We'll get it taken care of. You don't have a choice. If your appendix is the problem, it isn't as if you can opt out on having it removed."

"You're right."

He laughed a low laugh. "That's why they made me a doctor. I know about things like this."

Layla managed a smile. But it quickly disappeared. Was she alone? She didn't know if Gage had stayed. She hoped he had. She wanted to believe that he would be in the waiting room while she went to surgery.

Loneliness really did stink. She closed her eyes, trying to block the wave of emotion that competed in the pain of her abdomen. A nurse apologized, as if she had done something. Layla mumbled that it was okay.

After all, wasn't she always ok? This time would be no exception. She would get through this. She didn't have a choice.

As she drifted on the pain medication they'd given her, she thought about the hospital bills, taking care of Brandon, Christmas and Gage.

She dreamed about his hand on hers.

Gage sat next to the bed, watching as Layla fought something imaginary in her dreams. She kicked and moaned, whispering something he couldn't quite make out. Her surgery had gone well, but Jesse had told him that there was some infection because she'd obviously been sick for longer than a day. Stubborn. He planned on telling her that when she woke up.

Or maybe he wouldn't.

She didn't need lectures from him. She needed support. His mom had told him that when she called to check on Layla's condition. He'd asked his mom if Layla had family he could call. She had to have someone. Aunts? Uncles? People who could be there for her.

No one, his mom had assured him. So he had to stay. She'd said it in a quiet voice, but the meaning had been crystal clear. He was it.

He, Gage Cooper, the last person in the world to be there for anyone, was at Layla's side. Didn't anyone get it? He wasn't good at being there for people. He wasn't the person people confided in or turned to when the chips were down.

He leaned forward in the chair and watched Layla

sleep. Her brown hair was pulled back in a ponytail, her face was pale. He guessed he'd gotten better at being there for her. But who would take care of her when he left?

One thing was certain. He'd make sure she had support. It was the least he could do. He'd make sure her house was fixed up, that she had plenty of hay to get through winter. He'd also make sure Travis, Jackson and his dad kept Brandon busy.

He watched her sleep and thought about the two of them being apart. He'd keep riding bulls, wandering the country.

She would keep working two jobs, trying to make ends meet, hoping she could keep her brother out of trouble. Maybe she'd date. Someone would take her to Grove to a nice restaurant. Or maybe to Tulsa.

He rubbed a hand across his eyes. He had better get to sleep because he was definitely losing it. He glanced at the clock on the wall and groaned. It was almost morning.

Soft-soled shoes came down the hall. A minute later, the partially closed door opened. Jesse walked in, not looking much better than Gage felt. His brother smiled at him, and then at Layla.

"She should be out of here by this afternoon."

"That soon?" Gage forced his voice lower so he wouldn't wake her up.

"It's typically outpatient, but we want to keep an eye on her, get some fluids and antibiotics into her system, especially since she doesn't have anyone at home to really take care of her." Jesse gave him a pointed look.

"Yeah, I get it." Gage shot his brother a look that

he hoped stopped any speculation as to who would be taking care of Layla.

He would have said more, but he heard more footsteps in the hall, the soft whisper of a nurse and then his grandmother. She walked through the door a minute later, quiet, but observant.

"How is she?" Granny Myrna walked up to the bed, looked the patient over and turned to Jesse. "She's okay?"

"Of course she is," Jesse answered.

When had Layla Silver become the newest adopted Cooper? The Coopers had always tried to help her out. But in the weeks since Thanksgiving, things had changed. Gage guessed it was because he'd charged into her life, thinking he could fix his own mess of a life by focusing on hers.

And the whole family had gotten on board with the plan. Unfortunately they all seemed to have a different idea of things. He'd already talked to his matchmaking grandmother about that pearl-and-diamond ring she'd mentioned to Layla. He knew exactly which ring it was. She'd shown it to him about a year ago.

As beautiful as it was, he didn't plan on putting that ring on anyone's finger anytime soon.

"Get up and let an old lady sit down." His grandmother swatted his arm. He moved out of the chair.

"I needed to stretch anyway."

"You're such a gentleman." She sighed as she sat down. "Go buy your brother breakfast. I'll sit with Layla."

Jesse chuckled a little and headed for the door. "This all seems very familiar, Gage. If I was you, I wouldn't leave her alone with Layla. You'll be engaged by sunset."

Gage shook his head at the warning. He wasn't going to be the next Cooper to fall victim to her matchmaking schemes. "Gran, try to stay out of my business."

"I'm not even sure what you mean by that. But make sure you bring me a doughnut and coffee. Not a filled doughnut. I don't want pudding inside my cake."

"Yes, ma'am. And make sure you don't do anything crazy."

She grinned big. "Oh, Gage, you should trust me."

"Not even for a second." He leaned to kiss her cheek. "But I love you."

She patted his cheek. "I love you. And you need to shave."

"I'll do that later."

He walked out the door, and Jesse was waiting for him in the hall. "You know she's already planning your wedding to Layla Silver."

"I think she might want to scrap her plans. I'm not marrying anyone anytime soon."

"We'll see about that." Jesse pounded him on the back. "You're living in another world if you think our grandmother isn't already having invitations printed up."

They headed down the hall in the direction of the cafeteria. The hospital was still quiet, the halls still mostly empty.

"Gage, it wouldn't be the worst thing in the world," Jesse offered as they got close to the cafeteria's double doors.

"Maybe not, but I'm not ready. I still have a lot I want to do, places I want to go."

"I was heading for South America when Laura showed up in my life."

"I get that, but I'm not you." He sighed. "This is why I don't date in Dawson."

"Why's that?" Jesse pointed toward the buffet line.

"Because if you buy a woman a cup of coffee, this whole town has you married off."

"Yeah, I guess that does happen sometimes. But don't run from what you want just because the people in Dawson see it before you do."

"You're no help at all." Gage ordered an omelet and walked away from his brother.

He even tried to sit at a different table. Jesse laughed and sat down across from him. "Back to your old tricks of leaving when things get a little tough?"

Gage took a bite of omelet and ignored Jesse.

"You didn't used to be a chicken." Jesse grinned, flashing white teeth that Gage thought he shouldn't be so quick to flash.

"I'm not a chicken."

"Really? Because from my side of the table, that's how it looks. Something gets under your skin, makes you a little mad, or gets uncomfortable, you run."

"Stop." Gage kept his gaze leveled on Jesse, almost nine years his senior and probably in a lot better shape physically.

But Gage was pretty sure he could still take him.

Jesse wasn't intimidated. He laughed and leaned forward. "Or you'll do what?"

"I'll drag you outside and make you wish you had a doctor on call."

"I don't think you can."

Jesse pushed his empty plate aside. "I think I can."

The voice of authority boomed near them. "If you boys are through acting like kids, your mom is in Layla's room, and Layla is awake."

Gage looked up at his dad. "We weren't really going to fight."

"I figured that, but I thought I would warn you that your mother doesn't like getting bloodstains out of clothes."

Gage laughed, grabbing his tray as he stood.

Tim Cooper, best dad in the world, put an arm around his shoulder. It made him think about Brandon and what the kid had missed out on. What Layla had missed out on.

"You did good last night." His dad walked next to him.

"I did the right thing."

"Right, but people don't always choose the right thing."

Jesse took their trays to the dishwasher window. He fell in next to them and didn't comment.

Gage would have preferred the previous conversation, the one bordering on a fight, to this one. The one that felt like his dad was about to tell him the facts of life, and those facts had something to do with Layla.

Everyone wanted to give him some advice. Maybe someone could advise him how his life had gotten taken over by a pint-size female and her rebellious brother in just a few short weeks.

Chapter Fourteen

Layla didn't enjoy being told to lie down on her couch and stay there. But that's exactly what Gage had done when he drove her home from the hospital that afternoon. He'd carried her into the house, placed her on the sofa with an afghan and a pillow, then he'd taken off to feed animals. She'd used the time alone to do what needed doing. She placed an ad on the internet with a photograph of her mare. And then she'd cried.

She would have to pay the hospital bill and her loan payment. And she didn't know when she'd be able to work. Jesse had told her not to get in a hurry to go back to work, that her body had been through a lot and she needed time to recuperate.

What Jesse Cooper didn't understand was that she didn't have the luxury of staying at home for a couple of weeks. She had to get back to work. Now.

It wouldn't do any good to worry. She knew that. She knew it as she listed her house for sale, too. She knew it as she wrote down all of her bills coming due, and the amount of money she wouldn't make if she was off work for even one week. But Jesse had said to count on two. He'd prefer more.

The list of numbers on the paper brought a wave of fear. She crumpled it and tossed it on the table next to her.

"Lord, I can't do this alone." She closed her eyes and prayed.

She must have dozed because she woke up to the sound of soft snoring. She glanced over at the leather recliner she'd hauled home from a yard sale last fall. Gage was sprawled out, his feet up on the footstool and her dog sleeping next to him.

"Daisy," she whispered to the black-and-white border collie. "Down."

Daisy's tail thumped on the arm of the chair, and she rested her head on Gage's leg. Layla tried patting the sofa she slept on. The dog whined softly and curled her tail in close to her legs. Obviously she'd made a decision.

"Stop trying to take my dog," Gage grumbled, and opened his eyes.

He looked scruffy, and his green plaid shirt was untucked and wrinkled. Layla watched as he yawned and rubbed a hand over his face. Even scruffy, he was deliciously cute.

"She was my dog first," she said.

He grinned, sitting up a little straighter in her chair.

"Your dog likes me because it's cold out and she realized it's a lot warmer in here."

"Where's Brandon?"

"With my folks. They were putting up more Christmas lights, maybe cleaning out the garage. I don't know. He's fine."

"He has school."

"He came home, packed a bag and he got his books."

"Oh." She didn't know what else to say. Gage couldn't stay here, at her house. Brandon couldn't move in with the Coopers. She couldn't continue to lose herself this way, to him.

"Are you hungry?"

"Not at all."

He lowered the footstool, and Daisy hopped down, shook and walked to the front door. Gage grinned at Layla, as if to say he had been right. She watched as he hobbled to the front door and let the dog out.

"My mom brought over some soup." He eased himself down on the end of the couch. "Jesse said you have to eat something. Chicken soup. I've heard it's good for the soul. I thought I might eat some and see if there's a change in mine."

Layla reached for his big, calloused hand. "Your soul is just fine."

"Is it, Layla?"

"Yes, I think it is. I think you expect a lot from yourself, and you expect a lot from God."

"I think I should go fix us a bowl of soup."

"I think I should get cleaned up and change clothes."

Gage reached for her hand and helped her to her feet. "I'll walk with you."

"I can make it."

"I'm sure you can, but I'm not going to let you." He wrapped an arm around her. "Lean on me."

"Thank you." It felt good to lean on him. Too good.

He left her in the hall. "I'll be back to help you. Do not go anywhere without me."

"You know you have to go home later."

He leaned in close. "I know. Mom is going to spend the night."

Her eyes filled with tears. Gage touched the back of her head, guiding her to his shoulder. She leaned in close and cried. She cried because she'd been lonely for a long time. She cried because people were good and kind to her. She didn't have to be alone.

Gage brushed his hand down the back of her head, stroking her hair. His lips grazed her forehead.

"I'll heat the soup and be back in a minute."

She nodded and walked into her bedroom.

When she came out of the bathroom a few minutes later Gage was waiting, leaning against the wall. He reached to slip an arm around her. She eased into his embrace. A long time ago she had told herself she wouldn't do this. Wouldn't let herself fall for the guy most likely to take off and leave a girl heartbroken.

But today he felt like the guy most likely to always be there. His arm around her was strong, and his shoulder was easy to lean on. At the sofa she turned to sit down but his arm was still around her. He pulled her close and ducked his head to kiss her. She wanted to tell him they couldn't, but her heart didn't agree. She very much wanted to be in his arms, kissed by him.

Loved by him. The thought shook her. His kiss shook her.

He cupped the back of her head and moved the kiss beyond a quiet moment. Layla grasped his arms and held on, needing this.

She didn't want to love him. But maybe she did. She knew the heartache in loving someone like Gage. She'd watched her mom, trying to hold on to a man who couldn't be held. She remembered her own heartache when Gage had used her to get to Cheryl.

She looked up, meeting the tenderness in hazel eyes that would be her undoing. Gage wasn't her father. She didn't think he was still the thoughtless boy she'd known in school. Time changed people.

"Stop thinking," he whispered close to her ear as he nuzzled her cheek.

"I have to, Gage. I don't get to not think."

"You think too much." He trailed kisses from her cheek, back to her mouth.

She had to be responsible. She had Brandon. She knew how the wrong choices could tear a person's life apart.

She leaned in to his shoulder and then slowly drew back, pulling out of his arms. "I have to think."

"I know." He brushed strands of hair, tucking them behind her ear.

She sat hard on the sofa and reached for the afghan that she'd left on the back of the couch. She needed to think, but she couldn't.

Gage smiled down at her. "I'm going to get you that bowl of soup."

"Thank you." Maybe if he left the room she could put two thoughts together and make sense of what seemed to be happening.

Car headlights flashed through the window. Layla looked at Gage and he shrugged. "I'd say that's my mom or Granny Myrna. Either way, we're busted."

"Busted? For what?"

He winked at her. "For that kiss."

"They didn't see."

"No, but they have mom radar. I bet they know. Don't worry, though—I don't kiss and tell."

"You're horrible."

He tipped his hat. "Now you're catching on. I'm no-body's hero, Layla."

"I didn't think you were."

He laughed as he walked into the kitchen. And she smiled, because as much as he twisted her inside out and made her question everything, he also made smiling easier than it had been in a long time.

His mother found him in the kitchen. She filled a cup with water and placed it in the microwave, then turned to look at him. He squirmed a little. It was the same look she'd used on him and his brothers when they were kids.

"I didn't do anything." He found a spoon and placed it in the soup that he'd fixed for Layla.

"I didn't say you did. My word, you have a guilty conscience. I was actually thinking how proud I am of you. How glad I am that Layla finally decided to let someone help her out and that the person was you."

"Are you staying here tonight?"

"Yes. Brandon is here. He's getting a few things he forgot, but he'll go back to the house with you. He's pretty happy over there, but he's worried about Layla."

"I'm sure he is. They only have each other."

"It was quite a scare for him. We talked a long time after you left to take her to the hospital. He has a lot on his mind for a young man."

"I think they both do, and they're trying to protect each other by not discussing it." Gage picked up the bowl of soup. "I told her she has to eat something."

"Oh, I see."

He didn't need his mom reading too much into this. He was bringing a woman a bowl of soup. Soup. Not flowers, a ring or a lifetime commitment.

He shook his head at her, which only made her smile more. He walked out of the kitchen with the bowl of steaming hot soup.

"Here's your soup." He forced an easy smile as he walked into the living room.

Layla was sitting up on the couch. She smiled at him, then at his mother. But the smile was strained, probably a lot like his. He knew Layla was probably wondering how she could get rid of the people invading her home, her life.

"Eat your soup and don't argue. You're not going to convince us you don't need us here."

"I didn't say anything." She wrinkled her nose at him and took the soup. And then she smiled a real smile. "Thank you."

"You're welcome. I'm going to head back to the house but Mom is staying with you."

"Thank you, Gage. Thank you for everything."

She looked sweet and soft, curled up in an afghan, the bowl of soup in her hands. He wanted to kiss her again but he couldn't. He wouldn't.

He cleared his throat. "You're welcome. I'll see you tomorrow."

Brandon walked into the room, and Gage couldn't have been happier to see him. The kid was a great distraction.

"I'm ready to go." Brandon glanced at his sister and then at the door.

"Tell your sister goodbye." Gage reached for his jacket and gave Brandon a shove in the right direction.

Brandon looked at the ground and then at Layla. And then he hurried forward, gave her a quick hug and out the door he went.

Layla smiled a weepy smile that sent Gage out the door as quickly as her brother. He met up with Brandon out by his truck. The kid looked red in the face, like he might make a run for it.

"She's going to be okay, you know," Gage offered as he pulled his keys out of the truck.

"She shouldn't have to worry all the time." Brandon got into the truck. They were heading down the road before he continued. "It's because of me. I've messed up. Last year I broke my arm and she had to take out a loan. And the roof needed fixing and she didn't have the money for that, either. Now she won't be able to work. I need to get a job, Gage."

"You need to calm down and remember that you're only fifteen and still in school."

"I've checked into it. I could quit and get some special permission to work. I could still go to night classes or something."

"You're not going to quit school. End of story."

"You're not my boss. You're just the guy who feels bad because you broke her heart years ago." Brandon glared at him in the dimly lit truck. "If you hurt her again, this time I'll hurt you."

"I'm not going to hurt her."

"Are you going to marry her?" Brandon's dark eyes were fixed on him, and Gage worried that the kid would decide to suddenly defend his sister's honor.

"I'm not planning on marrying anyone."

"Don't hurt her...that's all I'm saying."

"I'm just trying to help her out."

They were silent for a few minutes before Brandon spoke again. "She'll probably lose her jobs."

"We'll make sure she doesn't." Gage sighed as he turned down the road that headed to town instead of to Cooper Creek Ranch.

Brandon grinned.

He drove toward the Mad Cow. It was almost closing time but he thought he would talk with Vera before she replaced Layla. And he knew she'd have to replace her. Vera couldn't go even a couple of days without a waitress.

The parking lot was empty except for Vera's Jeep. Gage left the truck running and set the emergency brake.

"Stay here," he warned Brandon.

"You going to talk to Vera about Layla's job?"

"I reckon I am."

Brandon grinned again. The kid was getting as bad as Gage's mom and Granny Myrna. When Gage walked through the door of the little café, the cowbell over the door clanged, and Vera looked up from the cash register.

"Didn't you see the Closed sign?" Vera smiled, making it okay to be there at closing time. She glanced at her register tape and then raised her gaze to his again.

"You know me, Vera, no sense of time and no respect for rules." He pushed his hat back and grinned at her, not really knowing what he would say without starting a few new rumors.

"You're going to have to come up with something

better than that." She pulled off her reading glasses and let them hang from the chain on her neck. "So?"

"I just wondered…" He looked around at the empty dining room. He could hear someone in the kitchen rattling dishes and singing to the radio. He cleared his throat and thought about that pile of bills he'd seen while he'd been watching Layla sleep.

"You was wondering?"

He cleared his throat. "About Layla's job."

Vera pinned him with a look. "I'm going to have to hire someone, Gage. I'd do it myself if I had more hands and a lot more energy, but I don't."

"She's worried about it."

"I'm sure she is. This is going to be hard on her in a lot of ways. I'm just not sure what I can do. The job I gave her was temporary while my other girl is out having her baby. Now I've got Layla out."

"I'll do the job for her while she's gone. We can set up an account for the tips I earn and give it to her."

The words were out before he could stop himself. What in the world would people say? So much for keeping Dawson out of his business. Vera gave him a look, eyes narrowed and lips pursed but twitching like she might start laughing.

"What?" He crossed his arms over his chest.

"Oh, nothing. I just always wondered what you would look like when it happened." Then she started laughing, and he blushed from his ears to his neck.

"I'm helping out a person in need."

Vera's brows arched. "Of course you are, honey. I'm just saying, this is about the sweetest thing you've ever done. I'm not surprised, just real impressed."

Gage shifted from foot to foot and adjusted his hat. "Well, I should go."

"Don't you want to know your hours?" She laughed a little more. "What about the feed store? Are they going to replace her?"

He'd forgotten about the feed store. "Guess I'll talk to them tomorrow."

"You're going to work her job over there *and* here? Gage, that could start some serious rumors."

"I know that, Vera. But people will just have to talk, won't they?"

"I guess they will." Vera came out from behind the counter. She stood on tiptoe and kissed his cheek. "She deserves someone like you."

"I'm not her someone, Vera. I'm just her friend."

"That's exactly what I meant. Now, you wait right here. I'm going to box you up a coconut cream pie for being so sweet. And I'll expect you here tomorrow afternoon at four."

"I'll be here." And for the first time since the conversation started, he managed to take a deep breath.

People were going to talk. There was no getting away from that. He shook his head and wondered what they would say that he wasn't already thinking.

Chapter Fifteen

Layla moved from the kitchen to the living room, cringing as she sat down. Her abdomen was still tender but she actually felt pretty good. And she was tired of sitting. Three days of being on the couch was enough. But Jesse had insisted she not do any chores outside, and definitely no waiting tables at the Mad Cow.

She closed her eyes and thought about all of the bills piling up and the money not coming in. She opened her eyes when someone rapped on the front door and then opened it. Angie Cooper had left just an hour ago, after fixing lunch and doing some housework for Layla. She'd had errands to run and promised to be back later.

The person walking through the door wasn't Angie, it was Gage. And he had a Christmas tree. He smiled as he dragged it in through the door, a big evergreen, the smell of cedar strong, filling up the house before he even had it completely inside.

"I brought you a tree."

"You certainly did." She wondered where they would put that big tree and how it would fit in her tiny living room. It looked to be about nine feet tall.

"It might be a little big."

"You think?" She laughed a little as he pulled the tree into her tiny living room and tried to stand it up. "We might have to move the furniture out."

"We might. But who needs furniture? A tree, on the other hand, is pretty important."

"You're right...a tree is definitely important."

The tree brushed the ceiling. He'd already shoved it into a tree stand. It looked as if he'd tried to trim it. One side seemed fuller than the other, the way trees cut from the field often are. It smelled awfully good, though.

"Do you like it?" He grinned, steadying the tree and looking from it to her.

"I think it's perfect. I do have an artificial tree we could have used."

"No way." He scooted it around the room. "Where do we put it?"

"Middle of the room? But that might cause problems."

"Hall?"

"More problems." She looked around the room. "The rocking chair can go in the kitchen for now."

"You're sure?"

"Positive."

He dragged the rocking chair out of the room and when he came back he moved the tree where her chair had been. It took him a few minutes of turning and positioning, but he finally had it so that the fullest side faced out. She enjoyed watching him work. He'd pulled off his coat and he wore a heavy, button-up shirt and jeans. His boots were a little muddy. His hat was cocked to the side thanks to the tree brushing his face as he angled it to make it stand straight.

"Perfect." Layla clapped her hands and smiled at him. She forgot everything but Gage standing in her living room with the perfect tree.

"Decorations?" he asked her.

Layla responded, "Attic."

"Great." He grinned. "Nothing better than climbing a ladder into an attic.

"It can wait for Brandon to come home."

"Nope, I can do it." He looked around. "How do I get up there?"

"There's a door in the ceiling of the utility room."

He headed out. She watched him go, and then looked at the tree he'd cut down for her. Any other woman would have been doomed by such an act of sweetness. But she knew his charm. She knew how easy it was to fall for that smile and the sweet things he did.

And yet, she felt her heart stuttering and stammering as it tried to convince itself that Gage Cooper had to be off-limits. For so many reasons.

A few minutes later she heard him banging and bumping around her attic. She waited, cringing at the vibration of her entire house. And then he returned carrying a rubber container full of decorations.

He set it down and swiped at a cobweb that clung to his hat. "For someone so organized, that attic is crazy."

She laughed at the description. "Yeah, I guess it probably is."

He arched his brows at her and pulled the lid off the container. He grimaced. "Is this it?"

"You were expecting more?"

"I don't know." He pulled out a box of lights. "Lights first. Do you feel up to helping?"

She was already on her feet. "Of course."

He walked to the back of the tree and started at the top. He strung the lights at the top of the tree, and as he reached to hand them to her, their hands brushed. And then on the next pass, brushed again. He moved around the side of the tree the final time, and smiled down at her.

"Almost done." He spoke softly, finishing the lights as she watched.

Layla needed to do something. She reached into the tub and pulled out a box of angel decorations. "These first. I always make sure these go on first."

"Are these special?" He took the box from her hands.

"They were my mom's favorites." She shrugged, trying to make him think that it didn't really matter. But it did. She and her mom had always decorated the tree together.

"Layla, I'm so sorry."

She looked up, blinking quickly to clear her vision. "Gage, don't. Please. Not right now. I wanted you to know they were her favorite. They're special to me. But I don't want to cry."

He tucked a strand of hair behind her ear. For a moment she thought he would kiss her, but he didn't. He ran his fingers through her hair and then he brushed a hand across her cheek.

As she turned to hang ornaments, her legs weak and her fingers trembling, he reached into the container and pulled out a box of homemade decorations. She smiled, remembering the year she'd made them with Brandon.

Gage looked at the baked dough decorations. "Also special?"

"The year after they died, Brandon and I made those together."

"Good memories, Layla."

"Exactly. That's why I don't want to cry. Each year I decorate the tree, I remember the special moments. It's more than just decorating a tree—it's the memories, the laughter." She smiled up at him. "It's corny, I know."

He shook his head. "Not at all."

They worked in silence, hanging each ornament while Layla thought about the past, about her parents, about the advice her mom had given her, sometimes at night while her mom nursed a new bruise and Layla's dad slept off another drinking binge. Advice meant to help Layla have a better life, but advice that had caused her to put her heart away, safely locked up where no one could ever hurt her the way her dad had hurt her mom.

Those memories weren't the ones she wanted. What they needed was Christmas music. She reached for the television remote and turned to a station with seasonal music. Gage started to sing along to "Silent Night." She sang with him.

Emotions tangled inside her, drawing her closer to the cowboy at her side.

"I think you should sit down." Gage wrapped an arm around her waist and led her back to the sofa. "I'll finish. You boss me around."

"That's a good idea." She sank into the soft couch and pulled the afghan around her shoulders. "Gage, you've been wonderful. I don't know how to thank you."

"I have a suggestion." He smiled as he continued to decorate the tree. "One of these days you'll agree to have dinner with me."

"Gage."

"I mean it, Layla. I want to take you out. Maybe to Tulsa. I know a really good steak house."

"I don't know."

He hung the last decoration, finding a spot that looked a little bare. "I do know. I know that we've become friends and I'd like to take you out."

"My life is really complicated."

"I know that."

"No, you don't. You've been gone a lot. You don't know how complicated it is to be working two jobs and raising a fifteen-year-old brother."

"You're right, I don't."

"I haven't been on a date in a long time. It isn't fair, to go out to dinner with some nice guy when I have all of this going on."

"Well, there you go. If you go to dinner with me, you're not going with a nice guy." He winked and then he dug around in the tub. "No star or angel for the top of the tree?"

She shook her head, trying hard to keep up with him, trying to understand where this conversation would take them and what she should say next.

"This is going to have to be a cowboy tree." He pulled off his hat and placed it on the top. "Perfect."

She had to agree. The tree was perfect. He was perfect, even with his perpetual five o'clock shadow and hair messy from the hat. He wanted to take her to dinner.

"Gage, I can't go out with you. A few years ago I tried to date, but it was too complicated. I work a lot. I have a little brother to raise. It's a package deal."

"I know that." He sat down next to her on the couch. He looked at the tree and smiled. "We did a good job. Now it feels a little more like Christmas in here."

"Yes, it does. The hat is a nice touch but you might want that later."

He shrugged, reaching for her hand. "I might. But I have others at home."

He lifted her hand and brushed a kiss across her fingers.

"Gage." She shook her head. "I can't."

"I know. When it comes to stability, I'm not the poster child."

"It isn't that." Not completely. The late-night talks with her mother came back to her, the warnings, the careful advice.

"I have Brandon, and he's pretty much all I can cope with right now."

"I know."

She touched his hand, tracing her fingers over his. "You have helped him so much."

"I'm not sure how." He chuckled, soft and husky. "It's not like I'm the best role model."

"You're a good person."

"Now I know you're making things up." He lifted her hand again, holding it against his cheek. "If you keep telling me that, I'm going to start believing it."

"Good."

He released her hand and looked at his watch. "I have to go. You'll be okay until my mom gets here?"

"Yes, I'll be fine."

He stood, looking down at her with a careful look. "Think about dinner."

She nodded. "I will."

He left. She watched as he pulled on his coat and reached for a hat that wasn't there. He brushed a hand through his hair and smiled back at her. Then he was gone and she was alone. She sat on the sofa looking at the tree, at his hat where a star should have been.

She thought about how it would feel to go out to dinner with man like Gage. She thought about how much Brandon needed him, and how it would break both their hearts when Gage left again.

Gage walked in the back door of Vera's instead of the front door. He didn't want people to know he was waiting tables until he actually walked out on the floor. Before coming to the Mad Cow he'd stopped at the feed store to talk to them about working for Layla, and they'd agreed. They needed the help, and Layla needed the money. It was a win-win for all of them.

Layla would be surprised. And probably a little bit mad.

"Hey, there's my new waitress." Vera stepped out from behind the grill and gave him a careful look. "You'll do, but you aren't as pretty as Layla." Vera laughed at her own joke.

"Where do I start?" Gage asked.

"I'll get you an apron and an order pad. You've eaten here enough to know how it works. You give 'em menus, get their drink orders and then go back to see if they're ready to order. My specials are listed on the board. Salads are in the cooler at the waitress station."

"I've got it." He followed her into the dining area. People turned to stare. A few of them called out his name. He waved and kept following Vera.

She made a big production of handing him an apron and an order pad. "You're ready for this?"

"Don't look so doubtful." He grinned as he tied the

apron around his waist and dropped the order pad in one of the pockets.

"I'm still surprised that you offered. This is a big deal, Gage. People are going to talk."

"I know." He looked around the dining room at the early crowd that had showed up to make sure they got an order of Vera's fried chicken.

"The Pullmans just got here." Vera nodded to a table with parents and two kids. "Go ahead and take their order."

"Will do, boss."

Ted Pullman watched Gage with a glint of humor in his eyes that Gage didn't really appreciate. "Gage, you're a waitress now? I knew cattle prices were down, but didn't think they were that bad."

"I'm helping Layla Silver out. She can't work for a while."

Mira Pullman smiled at that. "That's real sweet of you, Gage."

"Thanks, Mira. All of my tips go to Layla."

"You could just give her the check from the finals," Ted offered as he picked up the menu.

Gage had thought about it, but he knew she wasn't going to take his money. He wrote down their order and headed back to the kitchen. When he walked back to the dining room a few minutes later, the big table in the middle of the room had been filled. His older brother Lucky and his family, Jackson and his family sat down. Great.

"Hey, little brother, we heard you were waiting tables." Lucky leaned back in his chair and grinned. "How's that working out for you?"

"Well, I thought it wouldn't be too bad until I saw the Cooper clan."

Jackson touched his coffee cup. "Could I get coffee? And maybe you should be nicer. We're real good tippers."

Lucky laughed at that. "I'll give you a tip. Marry the girl. It'll be a lot easier than waiting tables."

"Thanks, I'll remember that." Gage walked off.

"Coffee," Jackson called out, and then his wife, Madeline, spoke softly, warning him to go easy. Gage glanced back over his shoulder and made eye contact with Madeline, who was one of the nicest people Gage knew.

At least he had one ally.

But he didn't have time to think about it. The Mad Cow got busy. He had seen it like this before, with every table filled. He'd just never realized how hard a job waitressing was until he was the guy facing all of those customers. Vera helped him out when she could.

Toward the end of the evening, he was doing everything he could to keep up with his tables. Vera laughed as he rushed out of the waitress station with a few salads. He turned to look at her and she pointed.

"Salads are better with more than lettuce."

"Of course they are." He looked down at the bowls of lettuce.

"You're doing great, Gage. My goodness, people are leaving tips in the jar at the register, plus what they're giving you. And Breezy suggested we have a benefit. She said she'd be willing to sing. But we should get a better waiter."

"Nice, Vera."

Vera held her hands up in surrender. "Breezy said it, not me."

The front door opened, setting off the cowbell that had never bothered Gage until he had to hear it over and over again. A gust of cold air came in with the newcomers. Gage turned, smiling at a couple that lived down the road from Cooper Creek, and then at Brandon.

How'd Brandon get to town? The kid looked madder than spit. Or maybe just upset.

"She put that horse of hers online," Brandon nearly shouted, catching several curious looks.

"Calm down." Gage grabbed the kid by the arm and pulled him toward the waitress station, knowing people were listening.

"She put her horse up for sale," Brandon said again.

"I didn't know." Gage grabbed his phone out of his pocket. "Give me the website link."

Brandon did, and Gage punched it into his phone while Vera shouted to him that he had an order up.

"Take that order to Jackson and his family." Brandon just stared at him. "Yeah, you."

Brandon grumbled something about not being no waitress, and Gage ignored him. The kid could help out, too.

While Brandon took the order, Gage glanced over the website until he found the mare. Great. Now what would he do? She couldn't sell that horse. He glanced out at the crowded restaurant. Someone had to buy it. She'd guess if it was him. But she wouldn't suspect Jason Bradshaw, and he'd just walked through the doors of the café.

Gage walked through the crowded dining room and

sat down next to Jason, who happened to be sitting with his wife, Alyson.

"I don't think the waiter is supposed to sit with the diners." Jason laughed, as he turned a cup right side up for Breezy to fill with coffee. She gave Gage a dirty look, filled the cup and left.

"Hey," he called after her, "you get what you pay for."

"What's up?" Jason poured a couple of packets of sugar into his coffee.

"I need you to buy a horse. Maybe pay for it and say you can't pick it up for a week or so."

"I don't want to buy a horse."

"I'll pay for it." Gage put his phone on the table in front of Jason. "It's Layla's mare. She must be panicking about money and she put it on this website."

Alyson sighed a little. "Poor Layla, she loves that mare. She has so much hope for it."

"I know. That's why we're not going to let her get rid of it." Gage felt like he was the only one getting it. "I'll write you a check, Jas, but you have to send her a message and tell her you'll put the money in this pay account, and send someone to pick the horse up."

"Why don't you just tell her you'll give her the money and she doesn't have to sell the horse?" Jason said it like it made sense.

"She isn't going to take my money."

"Yeah, she probably wouldn't."

"Not after you broke her heart," Alyson mumbled as she reached for her water glass.

"Thanks, Alyson, for that knife to the heart."

"She's one of my dearest friends. If you break her

heart this time, I'll do worse than that to you." She glared at him, and he knew she meant it.

"I'm not going to break her heart. Why is it if a guy does something nice for a woman, everyone assumes they're dating?"

"Well, when someone spends this much time with a woman, it looks like a relationship."

Gage tapped his phone screen. "Do you have that website?"

Jason picked up his own phone and typed it in. "I'll buy the horse, Gage. And you bring me the check tomorrow. But you'd better listen to my wife."

"Yes, sir."

Vera came out of the kitchen, looking like she was on the warpath. He jumped up.

"Are you working for me or not?" She glanced from Gage to the crowded dining room.

"I'm working. I had to take care of an emergency."

"There's a fifteen-year-old kid carrying orders to customers," Vera informed him. "And he's doing a better job than you."

Jason laughed.

"Yeah, well, I'm injured." Gage pointed to his braced knee. "I'm supposed to rest a lot."

"You've been resting all your life. Now get to work." Vera handed him the coffeepot. "Fill up some cups and remember why you're doing this."

How could he forget? As he filled up coffee cups, he tried to guess Layla's reaction when she found out he'd bought her horse. She'd be mad. Really mad. Or she'd love him forever.

He didn't know how to feel about that. People wanted to order, and others were waiting for drinks to be refilled. When he'd come home for the holidays, he hadn't expected his life to get tangled up with Layla Silver's. But now that it was, how did he get it untangled?

And did he want to?

Chapter Sixteen

On Friday the new owner picked up Pretty Girl. Layla stood on her front porch and cried as the mare drove away. A week from Christmas, at least she had a nice check that would keep her from defaulting on the bank loan. She wiped at the tears streaming down her cheeks. She had to stop crying because crying wouldn't make it any better.

Telling herself that never seemed to work. Sometimes a girl just needed a good cry. Especially when her horse was being trailered down the drive, whinnying as she got farther and farther from home.

Layla had to go inside, away from the heartbreaking sound. Daisy sat next to her, whining and nuzzling Layla's hand with her cold nose. She brushed her hand through the soft fur at the collie's neck.

Beth would come by any minute. She had called earlier. Now that Layla was feeling better, Beth wanted to take her to the community center. They were putting finishing touches on the Living Nativity that would take place the following weekend, right before Christmas.

After watching the rehearsal, they would head to the Mad Cow for dinner.

Layla slipped off her barn boots and put on suede boots that had a warm lining. She grabbed her jacket off the hook next to the door just as Beth's truck pulled up the drive. It was only the two of them tonight. Jeremy was caring for their son. Layla needed a night like this. She needed a break from the house, from people taking care of her. Not that it hadn't been wonderful. She had a freezer full of casseroles from neighbors and church members. She wouldn't need to cook for weeks.

Beth honked. Layla grabbed her purse and went out the door, not running as she would have done. Her side was still tender, and she found that naps had become her friend.

She climbed into the truck and smiled at Beth.

"You look great." Beth shifted into Reverse.

"Thank you."

Beth's eyes narrowed. "What's wrong? Did Gage…"

Layla laughed a little and wiped at more tears. "I sold my mare."

"Oh, Layla, I'm so sorry."

"It's okay. I mean, it's not, but it will be. I had to do it. And she's going to a good home."

"I'm sure she is." Beth looked away, and Layla wondered at her friend's sudden loss of words. But Beth wasn't a person to push.

"It hurt to let her go, but tomorrow will be a better day. And I'm hoping next week Jesse will allow me to go back to work."

"Don't rush it, Layla." Beth slowed to make the turn that would take them to Back Street. "Give yourself time to heal."

"I'm trying. It's hard to sit at home when I know that the bills are piling up."

"I know you're worried," Beth said as she pulled into the crowded parking lot of the community center.

Beth parked, and the two of them walked over to the nativity scene. The actors were walking through their parts. The animals milled restlessly in a pen. Layla watched as Mary and Joseph took their place in the stable.

The eternal story of the birth of a savior. Layla shivered in the cool afternoon, watching as an angel appeared to the shepherds in the field. She thought about what this story meant to her life. It meant faith. It meant believing in something more than herself, her own abilities.

If she'd only been trusting in herself all of these years, she would have given up. But God hadn't let her down. She had people in her life who were there for her, when she allowed them to be. She should allow it more often. This past week had taught her just how easy it was. It had taught her to be thankful for their help.

The Coopers had been at her side the entire time. Because of them, Brandon seemed to be doing better. Of course he would still have bumps along the way, but she thought they might make it through his teenage years. And because it meant so much to Brandon, she had accepted Angie Cooper's offer to spend Christmas with the Cooper family.

Gage. She hadn't seen much of him since the day he brought over the Christmas tree. Maybe he'd finally realized that he didn't owe her. Didn't have to make amends for something that had happened years ago.

It seemed silly, but she realized she missed him.

"Are you okay, standing this long?" Beth had walked away to talk to someone, but she returned, giving Layla a cautious look.

"I'm fine for now." She smiled at her friend. "As many times as I've seen this program, it still moves me. Makes me think about that night and how much God loves us."

Beth nodded, watching with Layla. The choir sang "O Little Town of Bethlehem" and Mary and Joseph greeted the shepherds who had come to see the baby Jesus. Beth looped her arm through Layla's.

"It's going to be okay."

Layla smiled. "I know it is."

"Do you want to go to Vera's for coffee and a piece of pie?"

"Sure." Layla answered as she was pulled toward Beth's truck. "Why not."

When they pulled up to the Mad Cow, Layla had a funny feeling something was going on. The parking lot was full, and almost everyone she knew was there. She got out, feeling uneasy, maybe a little sick.

"I think I'd rather go home."

Beth laughed and guided her toward the diner. "Not on your life."

As they walked through the door of the Mad Cow, Layla's feet refused to move forward. The restaurant was packed. Breezy stood in the corner with a guitar and a mic—and Gage. He was wearing an apron and taking orders.

"What's going on?" Layla looked around, managing somehow to smile and greet people who called out to her.

Vera walked through the crowd, her hair in its neat

bun, her smile familiar and welcoming. "Layla Silver, your friends and family put this night together to help you."

"I don't know what to say." Layla allowed herself to be led to a table where Angie Cooper patted an empty chair.

"Say thank you to that crazy Gage Cooper. I think he has a surprise for you."

"Why is he wearing an apron?" Layla sat down next to Angie.

"Honey, he's been working both your jobs for you while you've been sick." Vera hugged her from behind and placed a noisy kiss on her cheek.

"Working my jobs?" Layla repeated. She locked eyes with Gage. He winked, and she didn't have a clue how to act or feel.

"He wanted to make sure you had money coming in." Angie Cooper patted Layla's hand. "I think if bull riding doesn't work out, he'd make a fine waiter."

"He didn't have to do this."

"No," Angie said, "he didn't. He did it because he cares."

Layla wanted to argue, to tell Angie that Gage did it because he felt guilty. He felt like he owed her. But she couldn't. All of these people were here to support her, to help her. No matter what his motivations were, Gage had put this together. *She* owed *him*.

She closed her eyes and said a silent "thank you." Once again, God hadn't let her down. The people in Dawson hadn't let her down.

For the next two hours she sat at the center table, thankful but a little embarrassed by all the attention. People would come and go, stopping to talk with her for a few minutes, to hug her, to tell her that she was strong and they all admired her.

Toward the end of the evening, Angie rubbed her back a little. "Why don't you let Gage take you home? You look exhausted. This was probably too much for one day."

"No, I'm fine. And Beth can take me."

"Beth left thirty minutes ago, honey. I think she even said goodbye to you." She looked around the room. She was right. Beth was gone.

Layla hadn't even noticed.

Angie waved at Gage to grab his attention. He ambled over and pulled up a chair to sit close behind the two of them.

"I don't know how you do it, Layla. This is hard work."

She smiled at that. "It isn't easy."

"Why don't you give Layla a ride home?" Angie patted his arm. "I'll help Vera clean up."

Layla wondered if he felt cornered, as if they were being pushed together. He had to know people were getting the wrong idea. But he didn't look cornered. He shrugged and then grinned at her.

"I'm game if she is. Let me get rid of this apron and let Vera know the plan."

Ten minutes later they were in his truck. He'd insisted on warming it up before they left. Layla sat on the passenger side, wondering how it would feel to have her heart broken a second time by Gage Cooper.

"Were you surprised?" Gage glanced at the woman sitting as far from him in the cab of the truck as she could get.

"Very. Thank you for doing that. And for working for me." Her voice broke a little. "I didn't know."

"Because if I'd told you, you would have told me no, and mentioned that I didn't need to make up for what I did ten years ago. This wasn't about that, Layla. This was about me doing something for you because we're friends."

They were more than friends, but if she hadn't figured that out yet, he didn't know how to explain it to her.

"You're probably right," she finally admitted.

"Thank you for that. I do like to be right every now and then."

She laughed a little, and the sound was a relief. He wanted to reach for her hand but didn't. It didn't take a genius to see that she still thought he was only in her life to make amends for the past. Eventually he'd convince her otherwise.

"I'm leaving in January." That probably wasn't the best way to let her know he was feeling more than friendship for her. He was thinking about the future, and she played a big role in those plans.

But it wasn't quite time for that yet.

"Back to bull riding?" She didn't look at him.

"Yep. But before I go, we're going to that steak house in Tulsa."

"Are we?"

"Yes. We are."

She turned to look at him then. He saw the dark circles under her eyes, her pale face and the strain of a long day. He reached over and laced his fingers through hers.

"Do I have a say in this?"

"Are you going to turn me down?"

She unlocked her fingers from his. "I'm not sure."

He pulled up to her house. Brandon had gone home with Gage's dad about an hour before the event at the Mad Cow ended. They had a horse about to foal, and Tim hadn't wanted to leave her alone too long. These days, Brandon stuck to Gage's dad like glue.

Layla gave him a long look. "I'm not sure if I can do it, Gage."

"You'll be better by then."

"No, I can't do this. I can't go to dinner with you." She looked so sad he wanted to hold her and never let her go. He wanted to find a way to make her smile every day.

Somehow he doubted Layla was in the mood for caveman tactics.

"Why?"

"Because you'll break my heart." She opened the truck door. "I have a fifteen-year-old brother to raise. I'm not young and carefree. I can't do casual dating. You're gone more than you're home. This is it for me. This is my life. I raise Brandon. I work. I try to keep this old farm from falling apart. You go where you want, when you want. You date who you want and then you move on. And for a lot of women you meet, I'm sure that's fine."

"So going to dinner is out." She didn't get it. Maybe he should have told her that he had more in mind than a casual dinner with her.

He didn't get a chance. She was out of his truck in a flash, and hurrying toward the house. Stubborn female. He watched her go, deciding it was for the best. She needed to cool off, and he needed a better game plan.

Man, he'd never needed a game plan before. How did

a guy go about courting a woman as stubborn as Layla Silver? He headed for his granny's, because if anyone knew about courting, it would be Myrna Cooper.

He drove back to Dawson, glancing at the clock on the dashboard, and wondered if his grandmother would be awake. When he pulled into her driveway, the lights were still on.

He walked up to the front porch and knocked lightly. A moment later, she peeked through the curtains, turned the porch light on and opened the door.

"What in the world are you doing on my front porch at ten o'clock at night?"

He shrugged and stepped in, pulling off his boots before he walked into the living room. "Wanted to visit."

"I'd say I was glad for the company, but you look like something the cat hacked up, and you smell like fried chicken."

"Thanks, Gran. Can I sit down?"

"Take my chair and put your leg up while you're at it. You're going to end up having surgery again because you won't listen to a thing anyone tells you."

"Another compliment, thank you for that." Gage sighed, doing as she said, not because he wanted to, but because he knew she still had a flyswatter and she wasn't afraid to use it.

"Well, I can think of a few more compliments if that's why you're here. Like maybe you ought to shave once in a while."

"My self-esteem is tanking here." He grinned up at her, and he'd never felt less like smiling. His grandmother eyed him, like she knew what he was going to say.

"You are in a bad way. So tell me what happened."

He sat there on the sofa, wondering how exactly he should broach the subject of Layla with Gran. He decided to jump in, feetfirst.

"I told Layla I'd like to take her to a nice restaurant in Tulsa. She told me politely, no, thanks. Then told me I basically am just a good ol' boy, and she's got to think about raising Brandon and working to keep her place from falling apart."

"The truth is so hurtful." His grandmother fanned herself with a magazine, giving him a sly look. "She hasn't dated in years, Gage. Do you think you can bat those pretty eyes at her and she'll suddenly come running?"

"I'm not looking for her to come running. I'm looking to marry her." He choked a little because he hadn't expected to say those words out loud. To anyone. Now that they were out there, they kind of made perfect sense.

His grandmother couldn't stop laughing. "Oh, now, isn't that wonderful. But she thinks you want to date a little, then run back to bull riding and who knows what."

"Could you stop making me sound like a womanizer?"

"Are you one?"

"No, I'm not. You know me better than that. I'm not Jackson."

"Well, that ended well for him, didn't it?"

"Yeah, I guess it did."

They sat in thoughtful silence for a moment, letting his words sink in. He still couldn't believe he'd said them out loud.

"I have the perfect ring. Pearls and diamonds, so

very much like Layla. She's a gem, so quiet and beautiful, truly one of a kind."

"Yeah, she is."

"Don't monkey around, honey. She isn't the kind of girl you play around with. She's got a lot on her shoulders. You're going to have to make it clear from the beginning that you're in love with her and you want to marry her."

"After three weeks, I should just declare my intentions? That's kind of rushing things, isn't it?"

"I guess it is. You do what you want, but that's my advice."

Gage left his grandmother's with a diamond-and-pearl ring in his pocket. If a man was going to learn about all things related to love, she was the one to learn from.

Chapter Seventeen

Layla didn't have to drag Brandon to church Christmas morning. He was actually up before her, having fed the cattle, broken the ice in the pond and taken a shower. She hugged him tight before handing him a plate of bacon and eggs.

They had opened their gifts the night before. He was wearing the new jeans and button-up shirt she'd bought him.

"Sis, thanks for the clothes." He looked pretty happy.

"You're welcome." She sat down across from him with a small plate of scrambled eggs. "Thank you for the perfume."

He grinned at that. He'd used the money he'd earned working for the Coopers. "Mrs. Cooper helped me pick it out."

The scent was perfect—subtle, not too sweet or too overwhelming. She had thought he must have had help. She also knew the bottle of perfume cost far more than he could ever afford. But she loved the fragrance, loved her brother for giving it to her.

Christmas changed everything. Layla thought that

as they drove to church. She'd worried over the holiday, over money and gifts. As they pulled into the parking lot of the church she realized people had changed the focus of the day. The focus should still be a baby born in the manger.

The church wasn't crowded, not on Christmas morning. Many of the regulars were out of town. The Coopers were in their usual pew, along with the Bradshaws, the Johnsons and several other local families. Layla noticed the church had been decorated with poinsettias and twinkling lights.

Myrna Cooper waved her over, patting the seat next to her. Brandon and Layla slid in and sat down as the choir stood. She loved this, singing the songs that told the Christmas story, of faith and promises kept.

Layla closed her eyes as she sang, wishing the peace of this moment would last forever. She wondered why it didn't. God had said He gave peace, not as the world gave it. She remembered the verse: *Let not your heart be troubled, neither let it be afraid.*

Layla stood with the congregation to sing "Joy to the World." As she sang, Gage looked at her, making eye contact. She noticed the tears in his eyes, and her heart faltered. She had found peace during this Christmas service. Maybe Gage had found a way through his anger.

She smiled at him, hoping he would know that she understood. He had come home in more ways than one.

As the service ended, people stood. Hugs were exchanged, and friends wished one another a merry Christmas. Layla turned to look for Gage. He had gone. The door at the back of the church opened as people filed out, and she saw his truck pulling out of the parking lot.

"Ready to go?" Angie Cooper appeared at her side.

"Oh, yes, of course." Layla smiled, as if nothing had happened. She wouldn't be the person who heard a message and then quickly forgot what she'd learned. Peace, not as the world gives it. Peace coming down from the Father above, she reminded herself.

She turned to find Brandon. He was at the front of the church, and he looked strangely proud of himself. His smile seemed a little too big and his eyes a little too bright.

"What did you do?" she asked as they walked out the door and down the steps together.

"I didn't do anything." He looked young and sheepish. Then he looked over at Jade Cooper, with her pretty blond hair and her big smile. Great, the last thing she needed was her brother going girl crazy.

"She's a year older than you, you know," Layla warned as they drove away.

"What?" He sounded pretty surprised and a little puzzled.

"Jade Cooper. She's a sweet girl, and I really do like her, but I'll like her better when you're twenty-two and out of college."

He turned a little red. "Jade is just a friend."

"That's cool. Brandon. We haven't really talked about dating."

Brandon groaned. "Could we *not* talk about girls and dating right now? It's Christmas."

Layla laughed. "You're right. It's Christmas."

They followed the line of Cooper cars and trucks up the long drive to the big brick, Georgian-style home.

Lights were wrapped around the columns on the porch, and a big wreath hung on the front door. Layla knew it would be beautiful later, when the lights twinkled in the dark evening.

They parked next to Jackson. Gage's truck was nowhere to be seen. She tried to pretend she didn't mind that he had disappeared. He was a grown man. He could do what he wanted.

Layla walked up to the front porch. The Coopers were filing inside, laughing and talking. Layla felt her guest status keenly as she and Brandon entered the big house, taking off their shoes and lining them up alongside the others. Myrna Cooper had stationed herself at the entrance to the living room. She hugged everyone as they walked through. She hugged Layla tight and kissed her cheek.

"I'm so glad you're here. You are a pearl." Myrna held her cane in one hand and slipped her other arm around Layla. "You're a pearl, my darling girl. You're beautiful and beyond compare."

"I'm not sure about that, Myrna."

"Oh, Layla, I'm never wrong about such things."

The two of them walked arm in arm to the kitchen, where the Cooper women were gathered, putting the finishing touches on lunch.

"I should help," Layla said, but Myrna didn't agree. She kept her arm around Layla.

"You're still recovering. And look at the crowd of women in there." Myrna led her to a stool at the counter. "Sit down."

Angie pulled a beautiful beef tenderloin from the oven, then turned to her. "We have it under control.

I'm going to bake the rolls and then we'll have dinner. I think it will be about thirty minutes."

"Where is that grandson of mine?" Myrna asked, glancing at the clock.

Angie gave her what Layla would classify as a warning look.

"Do you all mind if I interrupt?" Gage's voice behind her surprised Layla. She turned, nearly falling off the stool.

Angie looked back, her smile big. "Well, there you are."

"Yes, here I am." He walked up right behind Layla. "I need to talk to you outside."

"I'm helping."

"No, she isn't." Myrna gave her a little push. "Go."

Angie echoed the sentiment. "Go. You have thirty minutes before dinner's ready."

"That's long enough. I hope." Gage reached for her hand and waited.

Layla slid off the stool. Gage didn't let go of her. He also didn't explain. They walked to the front of the house where she'd left her shoes and coat. All the while, her heart was doing a strange dance.

Gage helped Layla into her coat, his fingers trembling. He hoped she didn't notice. Trembling fingers couldn't be a sign of strength. She reached for the front door, but he stopped her.

"Not so fast."

Her eyes large, so expressive, searched his. "Why?"

"I need to blindfold you."

"I won't be able to see."

He laughed at the obvious. "No kidding?" He pulled a bandanna out of his pocket. "Hold still."

He wrapped the cloth around her face and tied it tight in the back. And then he took advantage of the moment, leaned in and kissed her. At first she hesitated, then she kissed him back, holding tight.

"Merry Christmas, Layla," he whispered close to her ear, smiling when she shivered a little.

"Merry Christmas to you, too."

He placed her hand on his arm. "Be careful on the steps. I'll help you."

"I trust you."

"Good. Okay, step." He allowed her to go slow. "Next step. And two more."

He led her down the sidewalk. The sun was warm and the breeze had calmed down. Snow would have been nice, but a guy couldn't have everything.

"Where are we going?"

"If I told you, it wouldn't be a surprise."

"I don't like surprises."

"I kind of figured you for a person who didn't like surprises. But I promise, you'll like this one."

They stopped walking. She stood still, her hand still on his. "Gage?"

"Hold on." He stepped away from her.

"Gage?"

"Give me a second." He untied the mare, adjusted the big bow around her neck and led her close to Layla. He slipped the lead rope into her hand, then stepped behind her to untie the bandanna.

When it dropped, she gave a gasp that turned to a sob. And then she hugged the mare's neck. He stood behind her as she ran her hands across the horse's face, then hugged her again.

She looked up at Gage, tears streaking down her face. "How?"

"I bought her. I arranged for one of Jason's guys to pick her up, and I kept her there so you wouldn't know."

"But why?"

"Because you wouldn't let me give you the money, and I knew you wouldn't let me buy her and hand her right back to you." He brushed hair away from her face, then gently touched her cheek. "You're stubborn that way."

"It isn't stubbornness. It's strength."

"Yes, of course it is." He kissed her again, soft and easy, as the horse pushed between them. He pushed back. "Go away, Pretty Girl."

"I don't know what to say."

"Say yes," he whispered, waiting, holding his breath, wanting to hear that one word more than he'd ever wanted anything in his whole life.

Layla stopped breathing.

She held her mare in one hand, Gage's arm with the other. He remained close, his head touching hers, his breath soft on her neck.

"Yes to what?" she managed to get out.

Gage pulled back, his face serious, his eyes full of emotion. She loved his eyes. She loved his smile. She loved that when he held her, she felt safe.

"I guess we could start with you saying yes to dinner in Tulsa." He grinned as he said it. "You keep telling me no. But I think we have a misunderstanding."

"Do we?" She tried to keep up with what he was saying.

"We do. I think I failed to communicate my intentions to you, Miss Silver."

"Your intentions? How very Victorian of you."

"Not Victorian. Romantic." He leaned to kiss her again, and she held tight to his shoulders, the lead rope of the mare slipping from her grasp.

"What are your intentions?" she whispered as he held her close.

He smiled down at her. "My intentions are to show you that a cowboy can learn to stay home if the right woman is there to keep him close."

"Is that a fact?"

"Yes, it's a fact. Another fact is that when I asked you to dinner, I didn't mean I would take you out just once before I left town. I meant I wanted to take you out. And keep taking you out."

"Oh, like a steady girlfriend?" she teased.

"Stop talking, woman." He sighed and let go of her. He yanked the brace off his knee and tossed it aside. Before she could stop him, he dropped to one knee and reached in his pocket.

"Gage?"

"Layla, I love you. I'm going to court you, romance you, buy you flowers every day if I have to. And then I'm going to marry you."

"But…but…" She was so full of love for him, she was speechless. Her heart ached from the tenderness in his voice and his eyes. She reached for his hands and pulled him to his feet. "Stand up."

"I'm going to make it to a few rides this winter, then

I'm going to stay home and build a life with you." He stood and pulled her close again.

"What about Brandon?"

"We're going to raise him together. And my family will help. Layla, it's time for you to open your heart and let people help."

"You can't propose to someone you haven't dated."

"I've been trying to date you, and you kept turning me down."

"I'm sorry." She smiled up at him. "I haven't made this easy for you."

"No, you haven't. And you haven't said yes, either." He pulled back. "Come to think of it, you haven't said you love me."

"I do love you. I've always loved you. Since I was fifteen and writing your name in my notebook, I've loved you."

He reached for her hand. "My grandmother says you're a pearl."

She laughed at that. "She told me that just an hour ago."

"She said not to tell you that you're shiny, because a girl doesn't want to hear that she's shiny."

"What does a girl want to hear?"

Gage Cooper loved her. He loved her, and he'd just put one of his grandmother's rings on her finger. He'd bought her horse and given it back to her. He wasn't going to leave.

"That she's the only one in the world for a cowboy. That she's beautiful beyond compare." He kissed her lightly and whispered, "And that if this cowboy can't marry her, he's not sure what he'll do."

Layla touched his cheek. "I love you, Gage Cooper.

I do want to go to dinner with you. And I do want you in my life forever."

"I'm going to love you forever, Layla Silver."

Layla wanted to tell him that he had changed everything for her. She hadn't expected it that day he stopped to help her on the side of the road, but she was so glad he'd stopped.

Before she could speak, there was a burst of applause and cheers. Layla and Gage turned toward the house, where the Coopers were crowded on the front porch. Brandon stood with them, clapping and smiling big.

"Let's go have Christmas dinner." Gage held her close to his side.

"What about my mare?"

Gage groaned. "I didn't really plan the logistics of a horse with a big bow around her neck."

Before they could figure out a plan, Jackson was there. "I'll take her. The two of you oughtta show that ring to the family."

The family. Layla looked at the group of people gathered on the porch, including her brother. Family. She reached for Gage's hand as they walked up the steps into the arms and hearts of the Coopers.

Epilogue

Layla stood in the yard where her house had once stood. Gage had insisted on moving the little house, not tearing it down. It had a new foundation at the other end of the property. In its place stood a beautiful ranch house with log siding. Gage walked down the front steps, beaming at her. She walked to meet him.

His hand immediately went to her belly. "How's my little girl?"

"Boy," Layla insisted. Further argument ended when he kissed her.

"Girl," he whispered. "My grandmother insists it's a girl, and that we have to name her Pearl."

Their baby was due at Christmas, two years after Gage's very wonderful proposal. Her mare, Pretty Girl, whinnied from the barn. Andie Johnson, Ryder's wife, had turned her into a champion barrel horse.

"If she's a girl, we name her Pearl." Layla hugged her husband. "I want to go inside my new home now. You've kept it a surprise long enough."

"You'll love it."

"I know I will."

"Brandon will love it," Gage said, and they both laughed.

"If Brandon ever sees fit to leave Cooper Creek, that is. He loves staying with your parents."

They walked up the steps of the big, log home. The front porch ran the length of the house. They had designed it together, then Gage had taken over, wanting it to be a surprise and insisting it would be better for their marriage if he did the work and she stayed out of it. She hadn't quite agreed, but she'd let him think he was in charge. His sister Heather, who had decided to move back to Dawson, had taken charge of the decorating, and she'd run everything by Layla first.

The inside of the house was every bit as beautiful as Layla had anticipated. The walls were painted warm colors. The kitchen had everything Layla had ever dreamed of, from the hickory cabinets to the granite countertops, to the stone flooring.

"It's beautiful."

Gage hugged her close. "Mrs. Cooper, you're beautiful. I love you."

"I love you, too." She stood on tiptoe, kissing his chin, and then she grimaced. "Your daughter is going to be a soccer player."

She moved Gage's hand across her belly so that he could feel what she felt. He leaned down to talk to their daughter.

"I'm going to protect you and your mommy forever, little girl. And you'll grow up thinking you're a princess."

"You can't spoil her," Layla warned.

"Wait and see, Mrs. Cooper. Wait and see."

She couldn't wait.

*   *   *   *   *

Dear Reader,

I hope this book finds you all well and that you are preparing for Christmas with joyful hearts, and with a knowledge of Jesus that makes this holiday season special.

This story is one that has been in the making since the very first Cooper Creek book. Gage has been a favorite character. We've all watched him struggle. We've worried over him and wondered when he would find peace. Finally, in this story and at this special time of year, Gage comes home to Dawson and he makes peace with himself, with God and with his past.

Merry Christmas to you all!

Brenda Minton

Questions for Discussion

1. Layla Silver wants to do everything on her own. How has her pride helped her stay strong? How has it hurt her?

2. As Gage confronts his past, is he dealing with his anger or trying to fix things by fixing other people?

3. Layla's life has been turned upside down, and she has faced many struggles. What is the one constant in her life?

4. Angie Cooper told Layla to let Gage help. Why does she think she won't be strong if someone helps?

5. Gage is accused of trying to get right with God by doing good works. Do you think that was his motivation?

6. What situation caused Gage's anger with God? Why did that make him angry?

7. Why is Layla upset when her brother, Brandon, is so compliant for Gage?

8. How is Gage a surprising character?

9. Through the years Layla and her brother have been invited to spend Christmas with the Coopers and

other local families. Why does she resist those invitations?

10. Gage started helping Layla because he felt he owed her. When did that begin to change?

11. What changes took place in Layla as she started letting Gage in, and then letting other people in?

12. What did Gage have to learn about faith and God?

COMING NEXT MONTH FROM
Love Inspired®

Available October 22, 2013

TAIL OF TWO HEARTS
The Heart of Main Street • by Charlotte Carter

Pet-store owner Chase Rollins never saw himself as a family man. Can Vivian Duncan convince him to open his heart to her—and her baby—so they can build a future together?

REBECCA'S CHRISTMAS GIFT
Hannah's Daughters • by Emma Miller

Rebecca agrees to keep house for widowed preacher Caleb Wittner for the holidays—but never expects to fall in love with this man and his charming daughter.

THE FIREFIGHTER'S MATCH
Gordon Falls • by Allie Pleiter

As Gordon Falls' first female firefighter, Josephine Jones knows how to protect herself from getting burned, but can she protect her heart from the dashing adventurer who's trying to steal it?

YULETIDE TWINS
by Renee Andrews

Alone and pregnant, Laura Holland needs a friend and a job. When she turns to David Presley, she realizes the friendship she's always counted on could be the love she's always wished for.

SLEIGH BELL SWEETHEARTS
by Teri Wilson

Alaskan pilot Zoey Hathaway is in for the Christmas of her life when she inherits a reindeer farm...and one brooding, dangerously attractive ranch hand.

SEASON OF HOPE
by Virginia Carmichael

To help his community, Gavin Sawyer agrees to work with the Denver Mission. What he doesn't bargain for is falling for fellow volunteer Evie Thorne.

LICNM1013

REQUEST YOUR FREE BOOKS!

2 FREE INSPIRATIONAL NOVELS

PLUS 2
FREE
MYSTERY GIFTS

Love Inspired

YES! Please send me 2 FREE Love Inspired® novels and my 2 FREE mystery gifts (gifts are worth about $10). After receiving them, if I don't wish to receive any more books, I can return the shipping statement marked "cancel." If I don't cancel, I will receive 6 brand-new novels every month and be billed just $4.74 per book in the U.S. or $5.24 per book in Canada. That's a saving of at least 21% off the cover price. It's quite a bargain! Shipping and handling is just 50¢ per book in the U.S. and 75¢ per book in Canada.* I understand that accepting the 2 free books and gifts places me under no obligation to buy anything. I can always return a shipment and cancel at any time. Even if I never buy another book, the two free books and gifts are mine to keep forever.

105/305 IDN F47Y

Name   (PLEASE PRINT)

Address   Apt. #

City   State/Prov.   Zip/Postal Code

Signature (if under 18, a parent or guardian must sign)

Mail to the Harlequin® Reader Service:
IN U.S.A.: P.O. Box 1867, Buffalo, NY 14240-1867
IN CANADA: P.O. Box 609, Fort Erie, Ontario L2A 5X3

Are you a subscriber to Love Inspired books
and want to receive the larger-print edition?
Call 1-800-873-8635 or visit www.ReaderService.com.

* Terms and prices subject to change without notice. Prices do not include applicable taxes. Sales tax applicable in N.Y. Canadian residents will be charged applicable taxes. Offer not valid in Quebec. This offer is limited to one order per household. Not valid for current subscribers to Love Inspired books. All orders subject to credit approval. Credit or debit balances in a customer's account(s) may be offset by any other outstanding balance owed by or to the customer. Please allow 4 to 6 weeks for delivery. Offer available while quantities last.

Your Privacy—The Harlequin® Reader Service is committed to protecting your privacy. Our Privacy Policy is available online at www.ReaderService.com or upon request from the Harlequin Reader Service.

We make a portion of our mailing list available to reputable third parties that offer products we believe may interest you. If you prefer that we not exchange your name with third parties, or if you wish to clarify or modify your communication preferences, please visit us at www.ReaderService.com/consumerchoice or write to us at Harlequin Reader Service Preference Service, P.O. Box 9062, Buffalo, NY 14269. Include your complete name and address.

LI13R

SPECIAL EXCERPT FROM

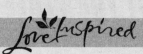

A shy bookstore employee runs into her youthful crush.

Read on for a sneak preview of
TAIL OF TWO HEARTS
by Charlotte Carter, the next book in
THE HEART OF MAIN STREET *series,*
available November 2013.

Vivian Duncan stepped out of Happy Endings Bookstore onto the sidewalk in the small Kansas town of Bygones. Watching leaves and bits of paper racing down the street, blown by a brisk breeze, she inhaled the crisp November air.

She hoped the owner of Fluff & Stuff, Chase Rollins, would help her put together a special event at the bookstore to promote books about dogs.

As she opened the door, the big green-cheeked parrot near the cash register squawked his greeting, "What's up? What's up?" He proudly bobbed his head and did a little dance on his perch.

"Hello, Pepper." Vivian smiled at Chase's recently acquired bird that was looking for a new home.

"Good birdie! Good birdie!" he vocalized.

"I'm sure you are." She looked around for Chase.

His warm brown eyes lit up when he spotted Vivian, and he produced a delighted smile. "Hey, Viv."

Smiling, he stepped toward Vivian. When she'd first met him, she'd thought he was an attractive man. She still did. At six foot two with a muscular body, he towered over her five-foot-four frame, even when she was wearing heels. His short, dark hair had a natural wave that sculpted his head. His nose was straight, his lips nicely full.

"What can I do for you?" he asked.

"I, uh…" Snapping back from her train of thought, she started over. "Allison at Happy Endings and I have realized books about dogs are particularly popular. We'd like to put on some sort of a special event and thought you could give us some guidance about where to get a dog or two for show-and-tell. I know the puppies you have are from the local shelter."

Chase ignored the bird. "The shelter is getting over-crowded, so I've started a monthly Adopt a Pet Day here at the shop. In fact I'm having one this Saturday." He handed her a flyer from the stack on the counter. "And I'd love to help you with your event."

"I'm glad." She was relieved, too, that Chase could help out.

"When you visit the shelter you'll have to be careful not to fall in love." His eyes twinkled, and his lively grin was pure temptation.

Vivian blinked. Her cheeks flushed. Had he said *fall in love?*

Pick up TAIL OF TWO HEARTS
wherever Love Inspired® books are sold.

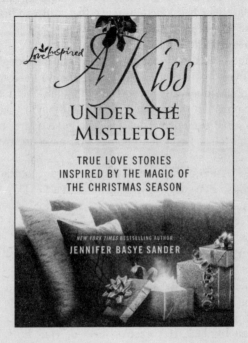

Christmas has a way of reminding us of what really matters—and what
could be more important than our loved ones? From husbands and wives
to boyfriends and girlfriends to long-lost loves, the real-life romances in this
book are surrounded by the joy and blessings of the Christmas season.

Featuring stories by favorite Love Inspired authors, this collection
will warm your heart and soothe your soul through the long winter.
A Kiss Under the Mistletoe beautifully celebrates the way love and faith can
transform a cold day in December into the most magical day of the year.

On sale October 29!

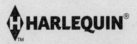